Tabletop Tales

Contents

The Tour
by Steve Dee

The guide led his party into an ornate room, the size of a market square. Marble pillars stretched up to the vaulted ceiling high above, and polished oak floorboards extended in front of them, towards distant stone walls, and large stained glass windows. The exhibits were distributed around the room at regular intervals.

"This is the Rahdo room," the guide said. "Please do not run through here."

He smiled to himself as he said this. Even though he said it several times a day, and even though nobody on the tours ever seemed to find it nearly as funny as he did, it was his favourite joke, and he enjoyed saying it.

"This room is a celebration of what is now referred to as 'The Golden Age of Board Gaming'; a period lasting just over twenty years, covering the end of the twentieth century and the beginning of the twenty-first. Nowadays, board gaming is the most popular leisure activity in the word, and it is difficult for us to imagine a time when this was not the case. The exhibits in this room however, hail from an era when board gaming was very much a niche activity, enjoyed by just a small percentage of the population. The games in these exhibits, ladies and gentlemen, are the classics. As well as still being popular today, these games formed the foundation for the modern board gaming phenomenon which, I am sure, you are all familiar with."

The guide began to lead his party in the direction of a large exhibit at the far side of the room. On the way he pointed out some smaller exhibits to the group, saying a few words about each of them, and slowing down to allow those who were interested to take a look.

"Displayed in this section, we can see some famous board game sets. In the front here, are the original prototypes for some of the most popular games ever. There's *Ticket to Ride*, *Carcassonne*, and *Dominion*, all of which have now sold more copies worldwide than all of the Harry Potter novels combined."

There were some murmurs of approval from the group, and a few people took out their phones and started taking photographs.

After a while, the guide gestured towards some paintings hanging on the walls behind the exhibits.

"As we move through the room, do please take a look at the museum's collection of original board game artwork. The eagle-eyed amongst you will have noticed original artwork from some of the beautiful games of the golden age - *Scythe*, *Mysterium*, and *Inis*.

We are especially proud of our collection of three of Marie Cardouat's paintings from the first edition of the game *Dixit*. They are titled *Planet Abacus*, *Floating Castle*, and *Post-It Note Attack*. The values of these paintings are unknown; however, one of Cardouat's other paintings, *Improbable Ladder*, recently sold at a private auction, for a figured rumoured to be greater than the gross domestic product of the Isle of Skye."

The guide paused. A few of the group had puzzled expressions on their faces, as though they were unsure what to make of this information.

The guide carried on, across the room, to the next exhibits.

"Now, we come to some games that literally, directly, changed the world. The first one here, is the actual *Pandemic* set that used to belong to Dr Jemima Dee, the pioneering scientist who famously cured malaria. In interviews Dr Dee always claimed that it was the evenings she spent at home playing *Pandemic* with her father, using this very set, that inspired her to enter that field of medicine in the first place."

The group gazed approvingly at the game, which had been arranged on a table as though play was about to begin, with some cities having one disease cube on them, some two, and some three. Two hands of cards had been dealt, and were face down next to the board.

After allowing a few moments for the group to take in the display, the guide set off again, and the group followed.

"Now, here we can see the copy of *Memoir 44* that was used in that famous game between the President of the United States and the President of Russia, at the end of the last decade. It is widely agreed, that it was indeed a great victory for world peace when these two world leaders decided to settle their differences on a cardboard battlefield, rather than an actual one.

A quote from President Winfrey was engraved on a plaque next to the game:

> *"I am proud that by choosing to avoid war, I have saved thousands, or perhaps millions, of lives. I am, of course, less proud that, in losing the game, I lost Alaska to the Russians. I can only apologise to the Alaskan people and say, in my defence, that I had no way of knowing that President Kasparov held a General Advance command card, and that nobody could have foreseen that he would roll those three grenades."*

"You will notice that this is not the traditional version of *Memoir 44*; a special edition of the game was created. The original version could not be used, because neither president thought it would be politically sensible for them to play as the Nazis."

The guide led his party up to the next exhibit; it was a marble plinth, on top of which was a glass dome, encasing a collection of hexagonal tiles. The tiles were three inches wide and an inch thick. Half of them were black, half of them were ivory-coloured, and each one had a line drawing of an insect etched onto its top surface. Hanging from an unseen bracket on the pillar behind the plinth, a 42-inch screen was showing a scene from a movie, in which two seated figures were facing each other, hunched over a small table, motionless.

"This," said the guide, gesturing at the tiles, "is the actual *Hive* set that was used in the recent remake of the film *The Seventh Seal*, which was, of course, the biggest grossing movie of all time at the box office. Many credit its popularity to the performance of Wil Wheaton, as Death. The former child star, right at the end of his career, won his first and only Oscar for this film. It was ironic, considering the role, that the Oscar was awarded posthumously. However, there can be no doubt that the decision to replace the original film's iconic game of chess with a game of *Hive*, shown in its entirety, in real time, also had a lot to do with it. Millions of *Hive* fans from around the world flocked to their local cinemas to watch the most intense game of strategy ever shown on the big screen."

The guide paused for a moment as the game being played on the screen reached its dramatic conclusion. The final piece, a mosquito, had been played. Both players were slumped down into their chairs, exhausted by the contest. The soundtrack began to build - a dramatic arrangement of drum and bass – until, suddenly, Wheaton, as Death, sprang to his feet and launched into a song and dance routine, in which he gloated about his victory. The lyrics to the first verse audaciously rhymed the word 'hive' with 'revive,' 'deprive,' and 'no longer alive.' The chorus rhymed the word 'confounded' with 'your queen bee is surrounded!'

After a while, the guide turned away, and added almost under his breath "Of course, the decision to make the film a musical comedy was not universally approved of by fans of the original."

As he shuffled forwards, his mind wandered onto recent developments in the world of tabletop gaming, now that it had become a multi-billion dollar industry. He knew of course that a lot of money changed hands to get *Hive* into *The Seventh Seal*, and the decision to do so had proved mutually beneficial for all parties concerned. Other Hollywood and board gaming collaborations, however, had not worked out so well, such as the fifteenth *Star Wars* movie featuring *Cosmic Encounter* being played by Stormtroopers on the Death Star. Or Daniel Radcliffe's James Bond forsaking poker and baccarat, in favour of *Sheriff of Nottingham*.

They moved on to look at other exhibits, and the guide spoke knowledgeably about all of them.

Eventually, the group reached the biggest one, at the far side of the room.

The guide was standing in front of a series of displays, in glass cases, of what appeared to be some sort of tribute to a primitive civilisation. There was unsophisticated artwork, and a collection of simple tools, and farming implements. Unexpectedly, there were also a number of photographs showing miserable looking men and women trying to build shelters out of sticks and leaves.

"In this display," he said, "we can see artefacts from the island of Catan. It is an island with a sad history. Previously uninhabited, it was bought by the German company Cosmodee Incorporated, and renamed Catan, after the legendary board game - the one which kick-started the modern boardgaming hobby in the English-speaking world. It was an advertising stunt, of course - Cosmodee ran a series of board game competitions, and the ten regional winners were each awarded joint ownership of the island, on the condition that they were prepared to move there and start a colony. These 'Settlers of Catan' sadly soon discovered that while they were all highly adept at playing strategy board games, none of them actually had the skills to build shelters, grow crops, or mine ore in the real world. The colonists were already starving, when they were attacked by pirates from a ship called The Robber…"

He paused for dramatic effect.

"…and now, I am sorry to say, Catan is uninhabited once again."

"That's everything we have to see in this room, I'm afraid. So when you're ready, please follow me downstairs to the role-playing game room, or 'The Dungeon' as I like to call it."

As they were about to leave, a young man at the front of the group put up his hand, coughed, and said "Excuse me. Can I ask a question?"

"Certainly."

"I have heard my parents talk about a game called *Monopoly*. Do you have an exhibit for that?"

"*Monopoly*?" said the guide, holding the young man's gaze. The rest of the group stared, in silence, waiting to see how the guide would react.

"No, I'm sorry. I've never heard of it."

***

An hour or so later, the tour was over, and the group had dispersed. The guide found himself with a little time to kill before the next tour started, and he decided to spend it in the museum gift shop. He usually spent his breaks with his nose in a novel, but he had recently finished the latest one he had been reading, *An American in Orléans*, and he needed a replacement; so he headed over towards the shelves of books in the corner of the room. He positioned himself in front of the section which had the title "Board Game Fiction," and began to browse.

His eyes scanned a few of the spines, and his brain rotated what they saw through ninety degrees, and converted it into words: *Agricola's Travels*, *The Gipf of Wrath*, and *1884*.

Then, he heard a voice to his right, saying "Have you read this one?"

The guide turned his head, and saw the young man from his earlier tour group, smiling at him, and holding aloft a copy of a paperback book.

The guide recognised it immediately.

"Yes, I have, but not for a long, long time."

He took the book, and inspected it. It had a picture of a green meeple on the cover, sitting on a brown leather armchair by a log fire. The title read *Tabletop Tales*.

"That's a very old book – it came out in the twenties, I think. Or maybe it was even earlier, I forget. It was actually one of the first examples of board game fiction; at the time it came out the genre did not really exist. If I remember correctly, it's an anthology of short stories put together by an English board game enthusiast. He placed an advert on the internet, asking for contributions from gamers who were also writers ... or was it writers who were also gamers... Anyway, this young man was a writer himself, and he thought it would be fun to be in the editorial role for a change, rather than the hopeful contributor role."

"And was it fun?"

The guide sighed.

"Not as much as he'd thought it would be. It was the first anthology he had ever put together, and it didn't help that he made a rookie error. He allowed all the writers to submit their work in different file formats, some of which turned out to be incompatible with each other; as a result of this, he later had to spend many hours going through the whole book again, putting back italics, headings, and line breaks. He was convinced that if he missed one, someone would dock him a star in an Amazon review. And would reviewers also hold it against him that some writers used British spelling, and others American? Some used the Oxford comma, others didn't. On these points though, he decided that if he didn't mention it, probably nobody would notice.

The real problem though, was that he did not enjoy having to choose between all the stories he was sent. Most of them were very well-written, and he did not like having to reject some. A surprising number of people wrote their stories on similar themes, too, so some had to be turned down just because they did not fit with the other stories. He hated having to say no to people – especially when those people were talented writers who had gone to a lot of trouble, all because of him. He even felt awkward doing his job as an editor, trying to tell people who were clearly better writers than him, that their work needed changes."

"He sounds like a bit of a wuss."

"Maybe. In the end though, he picked as many of the stories as he felt was right, with as broad range of different themes and styles as possible, and tried to stay out of the way as best he could. He also promised to share the profits with all the other writers, which made him feel a bit less guilty.

The stories he chose, in the end, were comedies, horrors, action-thrillers, and romances. They were set in the future, the present day, and a nostalgic childhood past. In other words, they were all very different."

"So, is the book any good?"

"Well I like it," said the guide, "but then, I'm biased."

_____

Steve Dee is an English board game enthusiast, and the author of a number of books and stories about board gaming, including 'Ticket to Carcassonne' and 'Hive: the Boardless Board Game.'

Traitors

by Dave Ring

"Alex is obviously the traitor, look at her face," Tommy said.

"That's something a traitor would say," I replied, sticking my tongue out at her. But also, I was totally the traitor. I slid a failure card into the pile. "Why would I be a traitor if the other two times we went to space everything was successful?"

"I believe her," Kay said.

"You always believe her," said Diega, who had apparently started dating Kay last week. She looked down at the rules. "Why do you call it going to space? We're technically Embarking On A Quest Amidst Intergalactic Cosmic Threats."

"That takes too long to say. See all the stars? We're going to space," I said. "And it's okay to believe me, because I always tell the truth'"

Tommy laughed.

"Now we know you're lying," Jasna said. She'd moved into Lucy's room a month or two ago. I didn't know her that well.

"Nope, Alex was right. She's good," Diega said. "The mission was successful." She fanned out five success cards on the table.

My heart sank. I must have put the wrong card in. "See?" I said to Diega, trying to keep cool. "You should trust me more."

Diega glanced around the table to see if the others were paying attention. When she saw they were distracted enough, she gave me a meaningful frown. Wait, was she the other traitor? I looked away. I'd thought Jasna was my teammate, but it could be Diega. Or Diega might be trying to get me to blow my cover?

I peeked at the other card that I had in front of me. It showed a glimmering nebula and a stylized argent crown. It was a success. That meant the one I'd thrown in should definitely have been a failure. What the heck? I looked on the floor but it wasn't there either. That ugly purple rug was gone too, probably recently. The floor it had covered was lighter than the rest of it.

Jasna was the next mission leader. I slid the success card face down towards her. She collected all the old cards and shuffled them together, then peeled off paired sets of successes and failures. That way nobody would know by process of elimination who had voted what. Although in this case, with four supposed successes, we should all have had failures in front of us.

"I'll be right back," I said. "Bathroom."

"It's at the top of the stairs," Jasna said.

"I know, I've been here many times," I said.

Jasna looked upset. Like, I think I saw her visibly count to ten in order to cool down. Diega and Tommy exchanged looks. I might have said it kind of snippy. I walked upstairs. It wasn't Jasna's fault. I guess no one told her I used to go out with Tommy.

The bathroom door didn't shut properly, so I flipped over the sign from 'aperta' to 'occupata.' While I was peeing, I noticed that my toothbrush was still in the cup with all the others. I also saw that the rules for revealing yourself as a traitor were on the radiator. Shit. Now everyone was going to think that I'd gone to the bathroom in order to read them.

I finished peeing and washed my hands. On my way out the door, I put my toothbrush on top of the trash. There was a massive bloody towel or something shoved in there. Disgusting.

Diega was waiting at the bottom of the stairs, messing at her braids in the mirror.

"Hey girl," I said. "Sorry to keep you waiting. You excited about the game tomorrow?"

19

"You should go," she said. "I thought this was a good idea, but it isn't."

"It's fine," I said. "I can play nice. Sorry about that earlier. And thanks again for making dinner."

"No, it's not that," Diega said. She grabbed my wrist, hard.

"Diega, where you at?" Jasna called from the dining room. I pulled my arm away.

"It'll be fine," I said, and pushed past her. Diega sucked at successful conflict. She always had to try and soften the edges of things. But not everything was meant to be easy. Sometimes you had to do things the painful way, and getting over break-ups was one of those things.

"Jasna still thinks she's the one," Kay was saying when I walked back in.

"No, come on guys," Tommy was saying, but stopped when she saw me. There was no way she was the other traitor, because when she was, she spent the entire game looking guilty and being way too quiet.

I looked around the room and met everyone's eyes. "Maybe I am," I said. Jasna sort of glared at me, but no one else reacted. "But if that's the case, I must be playing some real long game, because we've won the last three times now, and I got sent to space every time."

"I believe her," Jasna said, looking meaningfully at the others. "Let's play."

"Yeah, I do too now, actually," Diega said. She didn't sound genuine though. Like Jasna had made her say that.

"I really don't think she's the right one," Tommy said again.

"Right for what?" I asked. It was an odd turn of phrase. "My space team is always the best. Because we're not traitors. What happened to the rug by the way? I've always hated it, but now that it's gone I kind of miss it."

The four of them all looked at each other.

"We put it out back yesterday," Kay said finally.

"We got tired of it," Diega said. "We'll get a new one soon."

"You're not listening to me," Tommy said. "Stop changing the subject."

"Enough," Jasna said. That tone earned her side eye. Since when did the new girl get to talk to everyone like that?

"A toast," I said, raising my glass. I met everyone's eyes but Jasna's. "To old friends."

"And good chili," Kay said, looking at Diega.

"And to Malkama," Jasna said.

"To Malkama," the others echoed.

"What's Malkama?" I asked. It sounded like a new kind of yoga.

"It's a house thing," Jasna said. "You're the captain, Alex. Suggest a team."

I got put on the space team again, to Tommy's annoyance. She was staring at her phone passive-aggressively instead of looking at anyone. But this time I wasn't going to wait for the reveal. There wasn't enough time yet for the traitors to win normally.

"Y'all are suckers," I said, as soon as it was official. I flipped over my identity card. "I blow up the ship. Y'all are dusted. Diega gets the captain token."

"You are kidding me," Tommy started to say. Then there was a lot of shouting. I laughed and went to the kitchen to eat some chili, which had been banished from the game table for being too messy.

"No one else wants more chili?" I called out. "It's super good."

"No, thanks," Jasna replied.

"Suit yourself," I said to no one, spooning another bite into my mouth.

"Alex, what the fuck? That's not what your card does," Tommy yelled. She was mad, but there was another emotion there too.

"Yeah, it is," I yelled back. I sipped my drink; the ginger beer burned my mouth just the way I liked it. I went back into the dining room.

"No, it isn't," Tommy said, her voice still raised a little. She looked at Jasna.

"Look at this symbol," Jasna said. There was a little snake symbol in the corner.

"What the heck does that mean? Is it an expansion or something?" I asked.

Diega had the rules out. "If the traitor card has the snake symbol on it, they must shed their skin and take a new identity card from the gold deck after performing their secret traitor action."

"I've never heard that rule. What book is it in?" I asked.

Diega held up the rules; they looked like the regular core ones.

"Honestly, I've never heard of this rule. Has anyone else?" I looked around the table.

"What? By the way, drink and potty break," Jasna asked on her way to the kitchen. "I'll get you another one, Alex."

"Sure," I said. Mine was just about empty. I threw it back.

"Get me a beer?" Kay called after Jasna.

"Where's the gold deck? Can I see those?" I asked Diega, but she ignored me. "Since when are there these extra rules?"

"We're playing a special legacy version," Jasna said, coming back in. "We opened it last night. Deena was over. You have to read special rules when different things happen."

She handed me my drink and cleaned up my empty glass. I took a sip.

"Oh yeah?" I said. "Too bad she didn't come over tonight. I like Deena a lot." Deena was beautiful too. We'd made out at Citybar the previous week. It probably would have been weird to hang with her in front of Tommy though.

"How do you know Deena?" I asked Jasna.

She looked away and took off her glasses to clean them on her shirt. "I don't really. The others did."

"Deena was cool," Kay said.

"Deena *is* cool," Diega corrected, looking at me. Shit, did she know about Citybar? Me and Diega used to be a thing, like, five years ago, but I thought we were 100% cool now. Her and Kay weren't going to last, though. I could tell.

"P.S.," I said, trying to change the subject. "I definitely threw a failure in last round, but somehow it turned into a success? I have no idea how."

Jasna frowned and glanced at the big clock on the wall. It was almost midnight. I'd need to get an Uber in, like, a half hour, so I could sleep before rugby tomorrow. "It would have been too soon," she said.

"Too soon for what," I asked. "Are you saying you changed my card?"

"Actually, I did. I was trying to give you another chance," Diega said.

"What?" Jasna glared at Diega. "You shouldn't have interfered. It's important for everything to play out naturally."

"I agree completely," I said, crossing my arms.

"It doesn't matter now," Tommy said. She pulled a slim pack of cards from the box, still wrapped in plastic. "I think these are the gold cards." She unwrapped and shuffled them, then fanned the eight or so cards for me to pick one. The backs were like gilded H.R. Giger monstrosities.

"This is so complicated," I said, and plucked one from the deck. "What happens now?"

I looked at the card. My old identity had been the alien engineer, all tentacles and slime and bad attitude. This card was a regal snake-woman who looked like an empress. A massive cobra hood surrounded her face like a crown. There were chains around her wrist and a knife sitting on a tray in front of her. Hundreds of stars filled the black of space in the background. The Queen of Sacrifice, it said at the bottom.

"I had a feeling you'd draw that card," Jasna said.

Kay handed me a weird little blue light. "Shine it on the card. It'll tell you what to do next. We played this last night, too."

She took the dark and stormy from my hand.

"I was drinking that," I said.

Diega looked distant and serious over the pages of the rules. "Sorry, not anymore," Diega said. "It says the sacrifice shouldn't be too intoxicated."

"Yeah, okay. I'm not even close to drunk," I said. Although even as I said it, I felt a little woozy. Which was strange, because I had only had two drinks. I shone the blue light onto the snake lady. "Read entry 42," I read. "And open box J."

"The other players, including the traitor's former comrade, are now on one team against the snake traitor," Diega kept reading. "Remove the knife from the box and perform the ritual as described in entry 468, dedicating the death to Malkama."

"The snake's torpor should set in soon," Jasna said.

"Is that yet another deck of cards?" I asked.

"No," Tommy said, from behind me.

Kay opened a long thin package that she'd taken out of the game box. The thing she held gleamed in the light. She was looking at me carefully.

"I think you dosed her too heavy, Jasna," Kay said.

"The dose was perfect," Jasna said stiffly.

"What the fuck?" I asked. My eyes felt heavy. I could barely move.

"Make it quick," Diega said. "The instructions say that the death should be clean."

"This is getting weird, y'all," I said. "I think I'm going to go home." I tried to get up, but Tommy had her hands on my shoulders and I was really weak. What was in that drink?

"Weirder than you think," Jasna said and took the knife from Kay.

"For Malkama," Kay said, looking skyward. I'd never heard her sound so blissed out.

Tommy's voice was a whisper. "I love you, Alex."

Jasna struck.

I almost didn't feel it when she stabbed me; the knife must have been incredibly sharp. But when I looked down my lap was covered in blood. My pulse thudded heavy in my ear and my vision started going black. I could hear the others talking faintly. The lights on the ceiling shone through my eyelids like dozens of tiny stars.

"Grab her head," Jasna said. Her voice got more muffled in each passing moment. "We need her eyes for the next part. Does anyone have the sticker sheet? And move the cards so that blood doesn't get on them."

"Where's that towel?" Kay said. It sounded like she was miles away.

Then the stars snuffed out, one by one.

———

Dave Ring is the co-chair of the OutWrite LGBTQ Literary Festival in Washington, DC, and also the editor of 'Broken Metropolis: Queer Tales of a City That Never Was' - an anthology forthcoming from Mason Jar Press. Learn more about him at www.dave-ring.com.

Tabletop Mountain
by S.K.Dinning

Whenever the car turns the corner into the cul-de-sac, and our house comes into view, I always feel a small sense of trepidation. What will we find? What will Jamie have done this time, while we were out?

Surely it won't be as bad as the time he got hold of three tubes of paint, and used them to create a Jackson Pollock tribute in his bedroom?

Or the time he emptied a whole bottle of fabric conditioner into his pet guinea pig's cage, and another one into the tumble drier?

Or the time we arrived home to find Jamie had grown a beard? Well, I say "grown" - he had actually drawn it on himself with a marker pen. A permanent marker pen.

I should explain.

Jamie, my thirteen year old son, has what is euphemistically known as 'Special Needs.' Uneuphemistically though, he has a dual diagnosis of Down's syndrome and Autistic Spectrum disorder.

If you don't know what Down's syndrome is, I will tell you, but it probably won't help. It is the specific chromosome disorder that was identified by 19th century doctor John Langdon Down, and involves having three copies of the 21st chromosome instead of the usual two. There, I did say it wouldn't help, didn't I? Actually, though, I guess you probably do know what Down's syndrome is, so I'll move on.

I suspect you are more likely to be unfamiliar with Autistic Spectrum Disorder, or 'autism.' This is unfortunate, as it is really difficult to describe; nobody knows what causes it, and the characteristics associated with it vary so much from individual to individual. You might think you have an idea what autism is though, perhaps because you have seen it in a movie. If you have ever been a fan of eighties movies, you might have seen Dustin Hoffman in *Rain Man* and assumed, from that, that Jamie is a quiet type who enjoys TV quiz shows and is superhumanly talented at blackjack. Alternatively, if your movie tastes are more modern, you might have seen Ben Affleck's *The Accountant*, and concluded, from that, that Jamie's gifts are likely to be in the fields of double entry bookkeeping and revenge killing. Either way, you would be somewhat wide of the mark.

Let's not get too hung up on this though; you can always Google it later.

Jamie has many unusual personality traits that are probably due to his autism, such as needing a fixed routine, and having an obsession with doing jigsaws, and arranging random objects in rows.

Down's syndrome and Autistic Spectrum Disorder, are individually very different, but they combine (or at least, they have in Jamie's case) to give him a unique personality. He is without doubt, the funniest and most loveable boy I have ever known, combining a wicked sense of humour with a heart-breaking vulnerability. Everybody who knows Jamie adores him. However, I have to be honest - he is not an easy child. I said that Jamie has special needs, and it often seems to me that the main special need he has, is the need to be as mischievous as possible, at all times.

Jamie has the body of a thirteen-year-old boy (well, a thirteen-year-old boy who is small for his age) but a mental age far below that. He cannot read or write, and in fact barely even talks. Jamie's mother, Meg, and I, have been trying to improve his language skills for many years. It would mean so much to us to be able to talk to him, or even for him just to tell us something he cares about, but he does not seem to see the point. He will answer a question with a one word answer, and look at you strangely if you try to engage him in conversation.

"Did you have a nice day at school today Jamie?"

"Yes."

"What did you do at school today Jamie?"

Silence.

"Do you love your daddy, Jamie?"

"Yes."

"Say 'I love you daddy.'"

Silence.

I know that some of you are thinking - "that last bit sounds like a typical thirteen year old to me." And, yes, you might have a point there. However, Jamie genuinely only has a vocabulary of about fifty words. He uses those words to tell us (or anyone else who happens to be passing by) what he wants, such as "something to eat," "music," or "cuddle!" His favourite drink is milk – he drinks more of the stuff than a baby cow does - and he will often shout "milk!" when he is thirsty; unfortunately though, he usually mispronounces it as "milf!" which has caused a few awkward moments over the years when he has shouted it at strangers in shopping centres.

We love Jamie very much, but sometimes it is nice to get a break from being a carer. And so, every Sunday morning for the past few years, a succession of 'Personal Assistants' have come round to our home to help us. Personal Assistant (or PA) is the official job title given by Social Services, and not the one that I would have chosen; I think it makes it sound as though they do his typing for him, or pick up his dry cleaning, but no, they are in fact his one-to-one respite carers. They look after Jamie for a few hours, while Meg and I take his younger sister, Jem, out somewhere nice, to spend a bit of quality time together; time when we don't have to worry about where Jamie will throw his shoes if we take our eyes off him for a second.

Jamie, for his part, enjoys tormenting the PAs while we are out. For example, he is the master of creating a mess. His preferred tactic is to create a diversion – he might "accidentally" spill a drink, then while you are clearing that up, he will, say, empty the contents of a kitchen drawer onto the floor. While you are clearing that up, he might decide to take all the books off the bookshelf and post them back through the letterbox onto the front step outside.

We have tried many things over the years to limit the damage, and we have learned from our mistakes. We learned, for example, not to leave anything lying around in the garden, because Jamie likes to throw things over the fence and into the street. In the early days, it was any washing that had been left to dry on the line; so we stopped leaving washing on the line, and Jamie started throwing plant pots instead. When we started hiding the plant pots, the garden furniture started to go over. Eventually we cleared the garden of absolutely everything, or so we thought, that he could throw. We came back the next Sunday to find our fruit tree looking bare, and our neighbour, Dave, standing outside our house, waiting to ask us if we wouldn't mind persuading Jamie not to throw apples over the fence at his patio windows. Jamie had discovered that new ways to annoy people literally grew on trees.

One time we had come home to find the PA a nervous wreck. She was a retired schoolteacher named Sue, and it was only the second time she had worked for us; she told us what had happened, almost sobbing. It was the first sunny morning of spring, and Jamie had asked to play in the garden, so Sue had unlocked the back door to let him out. We had already discussed this with her and told her it would be okay, as the back gate was locked with a padlock. Unfortunately though, we had not realised how much Jamie had grown since he used to play in the garden the previous year, and he was now big enough to be able to climb over the gate, which is exactly what he did. Poor Sue had run to stop him, but was too slow, and once he was over the gate, Sue, in a panic, had not been able to find the key to unlock the padlock for a minute or so. She told us, her voice breaking as she did so, that she'd been terrified Jamie would have run into traffic. Instead, she'd found him sitting in the passenger seat of the car in the driveway two doors down, saying "Newcastle house please" over and over, to the bemused Dave in the driver's seat.

"It's where his grandparents live." I said.

I spent that afternoon putting safety wire on the fence and gate, to stop Jamie climbing over. But we never saw Sue again.

The story I want to tell you, however, the one I almost started a few pages ago, before getting side-tracked, takes place on one such Sunday. Meg, Jem and I were returning home in the car from one of our trips out. I would like to be able to tell you we had been to a museum, or an art gallery, or somewhere sophisticated; we did use to go to places like that when Jem was a toddler, but as she had become old enough to have input into the choice of destinations, that had all stopped. So, on this particular day were on our way home from McDonald's and Toys 'R' Us.

We had left Jamie with a very capable young man called Tim, who had been Jamie's PA for a few months.

Before leaving, we made sure Jamie knew that we would be back soon, and that his mummy and daddy loved him very much.

"See you soon Jamie."

"Bye."

"LoveYouJamie."

Silence.

"Do you love your daddy?"

"Yes"

"Say LoveYouDaddy."

Silence.

"Say LoveYouMummy."

Silence.

"Tim is here to look after you."

"Bye."

We liked Tim - he and Jamie got on very well, and Jamie seemed to respect him. There had never been any serious calamities on his watch. There had only really been one minor mishap - we had come home one time to find Tim wearing different clothes to the ones he was wearing when we had gone out. It was the middle of winter, but Tim was wearing shorts and a T-shirt. Apparently Jamie had turned the garden hose on him, and Tim had had to change his clothes, but he'd just had his sports kit in his bag. It was like the end of Pulp Fiction, but without the cool dialogue and the body count.

So, anyway, as we returned home on the day of our story, we were optimistic that there might not have been any major problems.

"Hi Tim," said Meg, as we went through the front door. "Is everything okay?"

"Yes, fine, thanks. He's in the dining room."

"How has he been?"

"Good as gold. He's been doing jigsaws for the past hour. He keeps popping out every few minutes to get another one from the cupboard under the stairs, but other than that I have hardly seen him."

"Great!" I said, and headed towards the dining room to tell the little chap we were back home. As I approached the door though, an uncomfortable thought entered my head - we don't keep his jigsaws in the cupboard under the stairs.

I turned the handle and pushed the door, which swung open to reveal Jamie sitting in the middle of the floor, surrounded on all sides by vibrantly coloured printed cardboard, which had been carefully arranged so that it formed a sort of carpet, which covered almost every inch of floor. Jamie looked up.

"Daddy!"

My hand involuntarily went up to cover my mouth, as I realised what I was seeing. They were not jigsaws. We don't keep jigsaws in the cupboard under the stairs, but we do keep most of my board game collection in there.

My eyes scanned the room from left to right. It looked as though Jamie had started in the far corner of the room, with *Carcassonne*. It was easy to see how he, and presumably Tim, would have thought that was a jigsaw - though admittedly not a very challenging one. I could not tell from my vantage point whether or not he had lined up the tiles so that the roads and cities were connected. I could tell however, from the impressive size of the medieval landscape generated, that he had not stopped at the base game, but had gone on to include the four expansions that, in order to save storage space, I had wedged into the base game's box.

Next to the lush, green, European countryside was, rather incongruously, the bustling marketplace of *Istanbul*. Next to that was the biggest (though not necessarily the most efficiently designed) *Quadropolis* city that I have ever seen. As my eyes panned across the room I also spotted tiles from *Fresco*, *Guilds of London*, *Downfall of Pompeii*, and *Ra*.

There were hexagonal tiles too, all expertly joined together, forming Japanese water gardens, new world colonies, and the island of *Catan*. I also noticed a few full sized game boards mixed in with the display - *Troyes*, *Viticulture* and *Concordia*. I guess Jamie had realised he was not going to have enough tiles to cover the entire floor, so he'd used the big boards to complete the tableau.

As my eyes crossed the room, my initial panic subsided a little, and I began to think that perhaps it was not the end of the world. Jamie does have a tendency to rip jigsaws up when he gets frustrated with them - he will make them fit by tearing off the tabs (yes, that is what the stickie-out bits are called - I Googled it) but that did not seem to be what had happened here - everything seemed to be intact. He must have taken a lot of care not to damage anything. This was going to be okay after all - it was going to take me a while to put everything away properly, but no damage had been done. Then, my eyes reached the pile of debris in the far corner of the room.

It was the empty boxes. Or, rather, it was a mountain of ripped up cardboard that used to be the empty boxes.

"Oh no."

To get to the contents of each box, Jamie had not removed the lids, like you or I would do - he had ripped the boxes open, as though he was removing wrapping paper from presents. Then he had thrown them, along with everything else that did not look like a jigsaw piece, into the corner.

I sank to my knees, and carefully crawled over the boards and tiles to the corner, to inspect the damage. It wasn't good. I sighed.

Jamie, meanwhile, was watching me with a concerned expression on his face. He could see that I was upset about something, but he did not know what was wrong. Usually on a Sunday morning (and most other mornings, to be honest. And afternoons), he would go to a lot of trouble to annoy the PA and/or his parents, but this week he had decided to have the morning off. He had just quietly got on with doing those unusual puzzles that were under the stairs. So why was daddy so distraught?

I leaned over towards the mountain of ripped cardboard and gave it a prod. There was a minor avalanche, revealing the remains of a few more boxes I had not noticed. Oh dammit – there's *Bruges* - it is out of print now and I will never be able to replace it. And – oh no! – *Splendor* is not even mine, I borrowed it from my friend Max.

"Oh, Jamie."

I put my face into my hands.

After studying me for a few seconds, Jamie, also on all fours, came crawling over to me. He put his arm around me and snuggled up to me. He kissed me on the cheek, and whispered in my ear.

"Loveyoudaddy."

———

S.K.Dinning is the author of 'Don't Let It Get You Down Syndrome,' a comic memoir about life with his disabled son, Jamie.

Errata

by James Redan

I stared at the board and the hand I had laid on the table. I still had options, some of them even good ones, but a lot depended on Kurt's next play. The light on the receiver faded in and out as it sat in standby - I checked the time. The atomic said 1205, and that meant dawn was underway topside. It also meant Kurt was a few minutes late.

While waiting for his call, I started laying cards down and moving pieces around. Checking possibilities, making up responses and counteractions. It was obvious we were approaching the end-game. Kurt had control of more than half the board, but I had managed to choke his flow of resources. If I could turtle up my front for just another couple of rounds, I knew he would start to feel the pinch. As long as he wasn't hiding some mechanized battalions or a hidden treasure somewhere, I had a good shot at resisting his push and flipping the advantage. The radio fizzed and crackled. A burst of static swallowed Kurt's voice for a moment, then settled to a low fuzzy hum. "...in. Copy? Over."

I started setting the game state back to the way it was at the end of the last turn while I fumbled for the handset. "I copy, Kurt. Still your move. Over." I set the handset down and waited to write his turn moves

43

in the game log. "....reinforce from Entiol to Kartro's border . . . spend four . . .ve. Over." The idea is to send the instructions for a turn to the other player, and wait for it to all be read back before committing. We want to prevent inadvertent errors on both sides; we only have each other and this game, after all. I called the move back to him, as I understood it, "Moving two units from Entiol to Kartro border, spending four move. Over."

His response was … annoyed-sounding, "Incorr..t. Move four units, spend ...or move. Burning Blitz-2 card. Over." Ok, that made sense. I was surprised he had a Blitz squirreled away, but using it now was a good move. I adjusted my receiving channel and boosted the gain a bit. After a few more back and forth calls we got to his final action for the turn, an all-out assault on my front from three sides and with unforeseen reinforcements. Kurt waited for me to get all the pieces in place, and then we traded blows - card actions and currency reserves, at least. His attack was devastating, but failed to push through completely. Still, he took out my hidden command bunker, thereby eliminating all policy bonuses for the remaining turns. I was looking at the final days of my empire. We signed off, and marked the time for our next contact, and my riposte.

There was an itch in the back of my brain as I began to sweep my defeated units off the board. It was when I went hunting for the play in Kurt's faction deck that it clicked. The Blitz wasn't there, and neither were some of the treasury cards he had thrown down. His play felt like a repeat of one of his early victories for a reason. I found it in the Log. Turn eight, almost exactly the same tactics; it was what gave him that crucial foothold in Kartro in the first place. Those cards were now in the burn pile. Unusable, non-refreshable, do not shuffle -- remove from play. I wondered where else he had been cheating.

Okay. Cheating is maybe strong. Mistaken, perhaps. Maybe he misunderstood a rule, or his logging was sloppy, or he didn't keep one for his own moves....or at all. That thought chilled me, I'd rather find him cheating than have him turn out to just be an apathetic player. I warmed the set up. "Kurt. Come in. Kurt, do you copy? You didn't have any blitzes left. Reset last turn. Over."

I gave it a minute or two between repeats. I think I tried for over an hour. I have no idea. At some point I became aware that I had been clicking the PTT on and off. In my other hand was a Blitz 2 card pulled out of the burn pile. I didn't even remember getting that. There was this metal box, like an old cash box with a slot in the top. All the burned cards went in there until a game was over. The radio had eaten a whole battery, and stood silent now. My throat was dried out. This was getting to me more than was rational. I sipped some water and checked the atomic. Fifteen hundred forty three. Well into morning. Going upside to hunt and scavenge might settle my mind, so I grabbed my travel pack. After a moment, I took my game book. The Log. The proof. It was a leather wrapped sheaf of bound paper I had branded with the coat of arms of my favored faction. Sometimes, devotion is uplifting.

The late morning sun shone green in the sky. Ash clouds moved in a great lazy spiral, forming a twisting sclera around it. Ozone and ammonia-scented air felt warm – stinging wherever my skin touched it. The pressure of the dust goggles and mask sealed on my face was reassuring and almost comfortable. I double checked that my air rifle was primed. It felt like a good hunting day, so I headed into the thickly shadowed knot-trees. Clearly I was lying to myself at this point, but I hadn't realized it yet. Hindsight analysis easily highlights the oddity of my behavior, but if humans could foresee the consequences of our future actions I don't think we would have had all those apocalypses.

Squearlers darted about the green-black canopy, chattering and swearing at my passing. They were generally too fast and cagey for me to get a shot at, so I ignored their manic anger. Probably tasted nasty anyway. All sinew and bone spines. I was looking for something more substantial, a feast to have. Some birds, or a small doggrel. My usual hunting pattern was a simple circular trudge around the entrance to my bunker. I could cover a lot of ground, but was hardly ever very far from home. This time, though, I walked dead away. Soon I was out of the copse and under the rad sun again. Moisture picked up from the mossy undergrowth steamed and sizzled as soon as I crossed out of the shade.

It must have been hours. Obviously, as the sun had grown and shifted to its blue flesh-devouring phase. That time, when I reached for my canteen, it had been empty. "That time," I say, because I don't know how many times I had reached for it. That was just the first time I noticed. I had become unaware of time. Lost in moves and counter moves and trying to relive the past actions to find other places where Kurt had not played RAW. The Log was in my hand. History laid bare, but still unclear. The raging sun stopped me from staying in that trap as even with goggles on and tints down my eyes were being burned in the light reflecting from the pages. I would find no more answers there, so I wrapped the book closed and put it away. Only then did I realize what I was doing. Far away from the bunker -- far out into land I had rarely crossed -- and that particular direction? I was marching straight for where I understood Kurt to be holed up. Did I have some half-formed idea of confronting him? Did I picture shaking my book in his face and demanding explanations? If I had stopped to reflect on my strategy with the same deliberation that I gave to the game, well . . . yeah, I'd be safely inside as the day fell away to likely death.

It was impossible for me to know how far I had come, lost in time as I had been. A few miles, yeah, but how many? Still, there was no way I would be able to make it back home without rest. There was also no way I could make it to Kurt without better direction. I dug my radio out of the pack, and turned it on. The portables only have a range of a few miles. Once the sun went down, interference would be less, but that thought was not very comforting when held up against the commensurate dangers of darkness in the barrens. "Kurt. Kurt. Come in. Assistance needed. Over." I repeated this almost reflexively as I walked on. After a while, I set my radio to work as a beacon. Transmitting an emergency tone every few minutes. When I got a response, if I got a response - well, hope is important.

The sun was beginning its final phase shift of the day. Aggressive blue that would scour unexposed skin to the bone was waning toward acid red that would cook you from the inside. I would need shelter soon. The ruins I had entered were only passingly familiar. I was crossing straight through a desolated city that I had only ever skirted the edges of before. These old remnants of civilization were uniformly dangerous, but not for uniform reasons. Among the reaching corpses of humanity's stolen glory there were glimpses of what I took to be the stony spires of the Vibrant Ones. If that is what they were, they were too far away to worry about me. Probably. In theory. With the sun turning red and the near-dark coming, I needed to find shelter. Torn walls stood eyeless gaping, but few cast the deeper shade I would need for safety. Some gaps in the rubble might prove large enough for me to scramble beneath, but there were no hidden places that would be empty once the near-dark came. The sun flickered in an accelerating syncopation as it approached the end phase of dusk. In the black intervals between the red and blue faces, I saw lights among the rubble. No people I knew would carry light outside, leaving only those I did not know and those that were not people.

Instead of going low, I decided to go high. A pile of debris lay in a drift against some twisted skeleton of an old thing. The top of it was maybe thirty feet, maybe higher. I picked and crawled my way up. At the top I slunk low in the shadow of the still taller decaying hulk and looked out into the dead land. I only had to wait out the sun's descent without getting eaten, and I might live long enough to worry about getting home. The red sun slipped away. Gazing out, I couldn't find any of the wandering lights from earlier. The radio chirped. It nearly fell away down the scree as I fumbled picking it up. Flicking off the beacon, I sat down to watch the sun creep away. A few minutes after the light was lost, the radio crackled in my lap. "I read you, Beacon. Beacon respond, please. Over."

It was Kurt. "I ," my voice cracked. "I read you. Is this Kurt? Over"

The pause was long enough that I started to worry, "Jay? Is that, Jay? What are you doing on the emergency channel? Over."

I explained the situation.

"Wait. Are you calling me a cheater? Did you walk miles, alone, into the barrens to call me a cheater?" Ok, he wasn't wrong, exactly.

"Well . . . no. Not . . . maybe you misunderstood the rule. Or forgot to burn a card? Look, we just need to talk about this, I can show the Log..."

"Yeah, no. You stay where you are. I'm coming to you, then you can explain it to my face." There was a pause of static. "Idiot," he amended. Again, I can't say he was exactly wrong.

I left it that, content to pick it up at Kurt's pleasure. I stared into the black featureless landscape for an embarrassingly long time before I remembered to take the tint glass off my goggles. This revealed somewhat more light than I had expected, the whole of the sky aglow with coruscating energy bands chasing through the upper atmosphere. Thanks for that, World War Six.

It was a minute or two before my eyes adjusted to the new light levels. I found the moving lights again, slowly among the ruins, making meandering paths with no apparent aim. They were moving generally in my direction, but with not enough deliberation to give me much concern. Still, it seemed stupid to let them get close enough to eat me.

I tried to reach Kurt again, but he didn't respond. I made myself as flat as I could as I watched the curious things wind through the dead city. Abruptly, their movements changed. The lights picked up speed even as they became more erratic. One or two disappeared, then more, then all of them were gone. There was something, though. A new sound out among the monsters and cannibals that I had been assured populated the surface of night. A buzzing, whirring sound that did not fit the bleak surroundings. Faint as it was, it was clearly getting closer, and I found myself wishing I could just turn myself off as well. The sound grew louder and closer until I finally relaxed. I recognized it as a light lectricycle. They were short range, but pretty nimble. I was just slightly envious of Kurt right then. He cruised into the wide rubble-strewn channel leading up to my scree hill. He slowed as he approached, apparently not planning to launch himself up to my perch. "Are you coming," he called out. I was about to respond, when I saw one of the lights reappear. That time, though it was much much closer. Instead of answering I simply pointed toward the odd thing. Kurt turned, twisting in his seat to be able to see back far enough. "Vibrant Ones." He pronounced it with a finality that spoke directly to what he thought our chances were.

I hesitated. The Vibrant Ones appeared sometime during the fourth apocalypse. No one knows where they came from, at least not anyone who shared the information. I didn't know much about them at all. Only rumors, or facts too risky to verify. They were faster and stronger than us. They hunt by scent, they prefer low light, and they eat anything. They are also basically human sized insects. I had never actually seen any of them, given their preference for fallen cities and my preference for anywhere else.

I checked to see if any were coming from other direction. Either the one approaching Kurt was alone, or whatever trick they used for hiding was working well. Not that it mattered, it was time to move. I took a route down the remains of the great thing that held up my debris pile. The bones were too smooth to climb up, but they offered enough purchase to keep me from breaking my neck on the descent. I mean, probably. Well, obviously, I lived, but I wouldn't do it again. I heard Kurt's lectricycle buzzing around to the side. He'd likely get me before I made it to the ground.

Fifteen or so feet from the ground, I saw Kurt do a hard bank and pull up beneath me. I saw flash of bioluminescent blue in the corner of my vision, but that is not why I performed a controlled fall onto the back of Kurt's machine. That was just a beautiful confluence of clumsiness and luck. He called me an idiot again as he sent us lurching backward. Two things from this, I fell against Kurt's back instead of the dirt, and the first leap from the Vibrant One missed us by a good foot or three. I grabbed on as I felt the lectricycle shift and surge forward. We seemed to be clear up ahead, but I could hear the sound of feet or claws (talons? spikes?) hitting behind us. Kurt accelerated, and I closed my eyes. He was dodging debris and detritus I could barely see, so I opted for total blindness. Most likely Kurt could not see those obstacles either. We hit something. The vehicle left the ground and began to twist in the air. We landed sidelong and sliding. I was thrown ahead, while Kurt when down with the ship. So to speak.

When I could lift my head, I saw Kurt laying with his bike pinning him down. It took me longer than I like to admit to pull myself together enough to get over to him. I kept forgetting that my wrist was broken until I tried to use it to support my weight. The concussion probably slowed me down too.

Kurt was conscious, but not great. I was trying to brace myself against the lectricycle and push it off with my legs, since I couldn't use my right arm. I had managed to lift it enough for him to start to drag himself free when something snagged at my pack and I felt myself pulled upward. There was that brief moment of weightlessness you get at the top of a ballistic arc before I was back down. My shoulder hit the dirt and I slid a few feet before rolling onto my back. A seven foot tall bug thing with too many arms and curving mandibles landed between me and Kurt. My pack was hooked on one if its serrated forelimbs. It held it up for moment, curious, before dropping it in the dust. Look, you don't survive rolling apocalypses without some fortitude and grit, so I rolled onto my stomach and got to my knees. If I was going to die, and Kurt was going to die, and we were never going to finish Sickle and Gold, I would at least do it upright and fighting. Okay, arguing. Whatever.

Between the two of us, Kurt must have seemed the easier prey, so when the bug launched itself, it was aiming to come down on him. I dashed forward; no, really - I can run. I dashed forward and grabbed my pack. I spun and threw it straight were I thought the monster would land, but continued moving forward for a follow up . . . angry yelling, probably. The Vibrant One landed next to Kurt and pivoted just slightly. Its forelimbs slashed together, completely tearing through my backpack. My supplies scattered out in the destruction. That completely took the fight out of me. That pack was made of stuff far more durable than my skin, and I could well picture having my insides scattered just as easily. The creature tilted its head, most likely to keep both of us in its line of sight simultaneously. Which is absolutely an ability bestowed on a horrible murderous bug monster by a just and balanced universe. It lifted one of its bladed arms above Kurt. I could almost feel its muscles tensing for the strike.

Then it just stopped.

It pulled the killing hand back and extended a smaller, more delicate limb. The Vibrant One leaned closer over Kurt while making odd clicking sounds, I could hear him begging it to leave. Senselessly, however understandably. It reached down and lifted something from the spilled contents of my pack. Plates on its head parted and I swear I heard it sniff. (I am aware that insects don't work like that.) It snapped its head toward me with more of those clicking sounds and took a small step, gesturing with the object in its hand. My Log book. The man-bug gestured at my log and then at me. I was probably staring blankly, or giving off confusion pheromones, if that can be done.

The bug-man gestured at itself, and then drew something in the dirt.

There was no way I was going to get closer to that thing. It pointed at itself (click click) and the drawing (click click). I would characterize its behavior as 'excited' if I were prone to anthropomorphizing horrifying insectoid monstrosities. It pointed at the Log (click click) and at me (click click). I sighed and moved close enough to be able to make out what fresh hell I was about to walk into. In the dirt, the creature had drawn a Sickle and Gold coat of arms. The next thing I did was simply the most rational course of action. I pointed to myself, and to the Log. I pointed to the creature and its chosen faction. I drew another coat of arms, for Kurt, and pointed to him. The bug, we call him Klicks, looked at me for a moment before coming to a decision. Klicks helped me lift the lectricycle from Kurt. Kurt helped me gather my supplies. Klicks returned the Log.

***

At the edge of the dead city there is a half building. The bits of roof provide reasonable shade and shelter. We installed a heavy table, some chairs, and an all-weather locker. Every week, come thorn-rain or rad-shine, we meet there. Klicks is a remarkably adept player, keeping me and Kurt on our guard. Never show your weak side to a Vibrant One, you will get wrecked. Klicks also makes sure that its kin don't eat us, which we appreciate. I maintain the Log. A new copy with all five coats-of-arms embellished on the cover, and it stays in the locker with a copy of Sickle and Gold. As for Kurt, on the first day we met there he showed up with an unexpected contribution. He had a laminated, pre-apocalypse printing of the officially produced errata. That Blitz 2 play was legal, and I had no shot at pulling a win in that last game.

———

James Redan writes down the things in his head in hope that they don't come true. Little is known about his origins or current life. This is not due to some overarching enigma, so much as a result of his failing to provide biographical information.

The Illusionist
by Dan Coffey

Jason was older than us by about four years. I'm
guessing, but I think that's about right. He had hair
on his upper lip, sparse and black, so old enough for
that. He might have been in the eighth grade. He
could walk to school, anyway, and wore a house key
on a shoelace around his neck. I don't know if he
walked to school, actually, there may have been a bus
involved.

That's how I remember him, though, not that I think
of him all that often. I can picture him coming home
from school, a red duffle bag slung over his shoulder.
He wore a zip up hoodie, blue jeans, and low-top
Converse Chucks. Pretty typical suburban uniform.
He was heavy and had the kind of acne that was more
big giant pimples than scatters of little ones. His hair
was brown and straight, but hung in conflicting
angles. So that's Jason.

His house, sort of this blue-grey late '70's ranch, was a
few doors down from Kyle's, which put it exactly half
way from my house, door wise. There was a turn in
there, though, to Kyle's cul-de-sac. Angie Jensen
lived in the next house over from Jason and I had a
crush on her. She was older, too, and looked like the
elf in the D&D Basic Set's Player Handbook. To me

she did, anyway, except her hair was shorter, about chin length.

It was her, anyway, that had lured Kyle and I to the curb in front of Jason's driveway. Or the chance of seeing her, really. She wore a key around her neck, too. Sometimes she would hang out in her garage and when she did we could ride our bikes in and ask about all the stuff her grandpa had stored in there, like the WWII plates with the little swastika on the bottom. He was in the European Theater from Omaha Beach to Berlin. I didn't care about any of that at all.

I kept glancing up from the D&D manual to see if she was coming down the street. Kyle was rubbing a stick to a sharp point on the concrete. He had a magnifying glass, too, to burn ants, but it was cloudy. Oregon has this kind of cloudy that never becomes rain, or anything, just hangs there.

So, when Jason appeared, making his way down the sidewalk, I didn't notice him because he wasn't Angie. Kyle didn't notice him either, because he wasn't a sharp stick or an ant. This was the first time I saw him, I guess. He had lived there for some time, but I never noticed before. This time he kind of just passed by, too, for that matter. He didn't say anything to us. He had a Walkman. He just passed by like we weren't nearly in his driveway and unlocked his front door.

A few minutes later, though, the door opened.

"Hey," he said.

Neither Kyle, or I, responded. I heard him, but just figured he wasn't talking to us.

"Hey kid," he said. "With the Dungeon Master's Guide."

"Oh," I said. "Yeah?" Kyle kept scraping.

"You guys come in here."

Now, this was a decision point. A few years before, that kid was abducted from the Sears. It was all over the news and stuff. It was like, your kids aren't safe even when you think they are safe. It changed things. Our parents were all like "Don't talk to strangers," and "Don't get into cars with strange adults." My sister said there were paedophiles who wanted to have sex with little boys and kill them. I was a little fuzzy on the logistics of the sex thing still, but killing was assuredly bad. I had dreams, nightmares really, I guess, about a guy rolling up in a white van and trying to snatch me. It was always a white van with no windows.

This wasn't an adult, though, and there weren't any vans involved. Or offers of candy, that was the other red flag. So no vans, no candy, but he was older, and we didn't know him, and he could have had all kinds bad of things in the house, and maybe could have wanted to have sex with us, or something. He recognized the Dungeon Master Guide , though, and in just a split second when he was walking by. I didn't even see him look at us. Maybe he didn't. Maybe he spotted it from up the street. This was important.

"Look," he said, "if you want to sit out there like a couple of renobs, go ahead, but I will give you one last chance."

So, in the face of potential death and dismemberment, we went inside.

We followed him down a short hall into a dark family room where there was a couple of couches and a coffee table. A few plants hung in macrame holders and there was one of those mineral oil lamps with a golden naked woman inside. Jason flopped into the smaller couch. He picked out a half smoked cigarette from an ashtray on the table next to him and lit it. He made a face after he inhaled, somewhere between pleasure and pain.

"Care for a fag," he said, holding the ashtray out. Kyle snorted. "That's what they call them in jolly ole England," Jason said.

"No," I said. "Um, thank you. I don't, ah, smoke."

"Suit yourself," Jason said. "Must be a paladin then?"

"I, uh, a what?" I said.

"You know," he waived his hand, "Crusader of the Holy Brotherhood. Defender of the righteous. Plate mail. A pal-a-din."

"I'm in Cub Scouts," said Kyle.

Jason leaned forward, smoothing his sorta-mustache, "Do you guys even play?"

"What?" I said. He jabbed the cigarette at the book which I was now clutching to my chest.

"Do you even play." He said it like deaf person this time, sort of messed up phonetically, and fake signed with his free hand.

"Oh," I said. "Oh, um, yeah. I mean, kinda. I got the set at a garage sale. Some of the pictures are cut out." I showed him. "They had rules on the back."

 Jason slumped back into his chair. "I see," he said. "Let me see."

I handed him the book. He flipped through it like one might a coffee table art book. He laughed to himself a few times and nodded. Blue smoke hung around him, churning as he turned pages. Watching him, I got this feeling like I had seen him before. Or, rather, the image of him there mirrored something buried in my mind. Not him specifically, I mean, more like something archetypal.

"They were tables," he said at last.

"What?" I said.

"The cut-outs weren't pictures, they were tables," he said. "They were making a reference sheet, probably. Don't have to flip through the book that way."

"Smart," said Kyle. "Then you don't even need the book."

Jason leaned forward. The cigarette was dangerously close to the filter. "Not smart, kid," he said. He slid his red duffel bag from under the table with his foot and unzipped one side. From it he took a hardback book with a robed man holding open two golden doors on the cover- The Official Advanced Dungeons & Dragons Dungeon Master's Guide. He placed it on the table. Little tabs had been added to the pages to mark important entries. "The books," he said, "are scripture."

I inhaled audibly. "Can I look through it?"

Kyle was watching the oil lamp.

Jason slid it towards me and then took it back. "Sorry," he said. "That's for DMs only."

"Do you have the AD&D Players Handbook?" I sat up, trying to see into his bag.

"You aren't ready for that, either," he said. "You guys just barely closed your Monopoly box."

I wanted a comeback, something that stung as bad, but I couldn't think of anything. I just watched him put the book back into his bag. He smashed the cigarette out in the tray. The motor in the oil lamp whirred.

"What you need," he said at last, "is a good set of training wheels." He stood up and disappeared down a hallway. When he reappeared he had a box, long and shallow, not unlike a Monopoly box. He placed it between us.

Dungeon!

"Sam, I already have that game," said Kyle.

Oh, I'm Sam. I forgot to mention that before.

"Psh," I said. "You have the board, which is covered in crayon and Elmer's glue."

Truth was, Kyle didn't care all that much for *D&D* , or fantasy, or even board games. He was more of a run around the cul-de-sac, or trap bugs in a jar kind of kid. He tolerated my obsession with a close eye on frequency and duration. Kyle had a sophisticated system of tit-for-tat checks and balances when it came to activities. Each hour of (my version) of *D&D* had to be repaid in kind with a game of hot lava grass, or whatever. It worked out.

Jason removed the lid, dumped sandwich-bagged pieces into it, and then took out the board. He opened it and placed it on the table. It was glorious. Different colored rooms clustered together, each indicating a difficulty level. TSR made both *D&D* and *Dungeon!* So, the art and references were all the same. Tucked in between the yellow fieldstone path were illustrations of monsters any self-respecting role-player would know: a troll, a black pudding, a purple worm. As well as the rooms, there were tantalizing locations, innocuous at the lower levels (Guard Room, Kitchen), but more ominous in the harder areas (Torture Chamber, Wizard's Laboratory).

"Wanna play?" Jason said.

"Yes," I said. "I would like that very much."

"Then," Jason said, "let the adventure begin."

I know this sounds totally stupid, but that's what he said. Let the adventure begin. Literally.

"We'll need to pick characters," he said. "The Hero is the basic one. He needs the least gold to win. The wizard is the hardest one, but he gets spells."

"Which one's the strongest," said Kyle. "I want the strongest one."

Jason shot me a look. I gave him a whaddaya-do shrug.

"What's your name again?" he asked Kyle.

"Kyle," said Kyle. "We're practically neighbors."

Jason looked back to me, "And you're Sam?"

I nodded.

"What do you want to be, Sam?" he asked.

"An Illusionist," I said.

"There isn't an Illusionist in Dungeon," he said.

"I know," I said. "I figured maybe we could make one up."

Jason tilted his head, squinted his eyes, and got a half smile on his face. "I suppose we could," he said, reaching for another cigarette butt. "I suppose we could do just that."

The three of us played *Dungeon!* every day for a few weeks. We added quite a bit of homebrew stuff, too. It was pretty easy to make cards that looked close to the game art due to it all looking more or less like a middle schooler drew it anyway. Kyle even bought in and didn't make me do something he wanted for an equal amount of time. *Dungeon!* must have been re-classified in his accounting system as a "mutual interest activity," like watching He-Man. Eventually, the training wheels came off, though, and we started playing *Advanced Dungeons & Dragons*.

That's right, straight to Advanced.

So, one Friday afternoon, a few months after we started, Jason was mysteriously absent. Kyle and I decided to ride our bikes around while we waited. It was nearing the end of the school year, and the sun was mostly out. At about seventy, Oregonians start to get hot. Maybe because of this, Angie's garage door lurched and then started to whir open. She stepped out into the driveway and waved.

My heart turned over. With all the *D&D*, she had slipped my mind. There she was, though, in a one-piece romper sort of thing and a big broad hat, like a person would wear to the beach. That's what she looked like, actually, like she was just headed out to the ocean. Her flip-flops smacked as she walked towards the mailbox.

I waited until she went back into the garage and then rode up. Kyle followed me, but just rode circles in the driveway. Angie sat in a high backed rattan chair with a red pillow, like a pearl in a clamshell. Next to her, perched on a plastic cooler, was Michelle Moraine, who everybody just called Moray, like the eel. She had big teeth and dark hair, so she looked kind of like an eel, if an eel could be sorta pretty.

Moray lived next to Angie, on the opposite side from Jason. She looked like Madonna, or like a girl trying to look like Madonna, anyway.

They had made a pitcher of red Kool-aid, which they were drinking from wine goblets.

"Hi Sam," Angie said. "Want some kool-aid?"

"Yes," I said. "Thanks." They poured me some, but it was in a Dixie Cup.

"So, how's things," Angie said.

"Good," I said.

"How's school," she said. "How's Mrs. Runke's class? She still make you do the bug collection thing?"

"We're doing it now," I said. "Kyle loves it. He caught a praying mantis yesterday. They don't even really live here, but I guess people import them because they eat aphids."

"Eew," said Moray. "Praying mantises are creepy. They have creepy eyes."

Angie opened her eyes as wide as she could. "Whatever do you mean?" she said.

"Creepy eyes!" Moray said.

Angie turned her creepy eyes towards me. "Do you like the bug collection project, Sam?"

"It's cool to see the different bugs," I said, "but I don't like killing them."

"Aaaw," said Angie. "You're so sweet."

I liked that she thought I was sweet. At school JPJ called me a wuss. He lived in the cul-de-sac at the other end of the block. We were friends, but he would turn on his friends from time to time. He really liked the euthanizing part of the collecting. He'd load his jar up with as many bugs as he could and then narrate dropping in the cotton ball of nail polish in a German accent. "First, I unscrew zee lid. Zen I admineester de poison to de cotton ball…"

"Sam," Kyle shouted from his circuit around the driveway. I looked. Jason was across the street, walking with purpose. It didn't make any sense that he would be over there. His house was on this side, after all. Kyle rode his bike over and hockey stopped in front of Jason. Kyle said something to him. They looked over to the garage. I waved them over.

Jason came up the driveway with a look on his face, like he had seen a Mind Flayer raiding his refrigerator in the middle of the night. He was extra pale, which made his zits even more day-glo, and a mist of sweat covered his forehead. The air of superior confidence had abandoned him somehow.

69

"Salutations," he said, shifting his red bag to the other shoulder.

"What?" said Moray.

"It's a smart way to say hello," I said.

"Salutations back," said Angie with a smile.

"Hello," he said.

"You live next door," said Angie.

"I know," he said, but not in a smart-ass way.

Moray squinted. "You do?" she said. "I haven't seen you. How could I not have seen you?"

"Especially with those glasses," said Kyle.

"Shut up, moron," said Moray. Kyle flipped her off.

"So are we gonna play," I said to Jason.

He seemed to get a shade pastier, if that is possible.

"Play what?" said Angie.

"Yeah, we want to play," said Moray.

"Girls aren't allowed," said Kyle, balancing on his pedals.

"That's not true," I said. "Girls play D and D. It's on the commercial."

"What's D and D," said Angie.

Jason didn't move for a few seconds. He just stood there and sweated. It stands out in my memory like it was a sort of painting. Kyle balancing on his bike, Angie on her clam shell, Morey leaning forward with her teeth, me hanging on for Jason's response, and Jason standing there sweating.

"I, uh," he said. "It's a game."

"Like Monopoly?" said Angie.

Jason couldn't control a scoff at that. "No," he said. "It's a fantasy role-playing game. There's no board, or cards, or anything like that."

"You make a character," I chimed in. "Like I am Paj'di, a half-elf Illusionist."

"Sounds like a girl name, Paj'di," said Moray.

"It is," I said. "You can be anything you want," said Jason.

"I'm a fighter," said Kyle. "A guy fighter," he clarified.

"What are you," said Angie to Jason.

"I'm the Dungeon Master. I don't have a character. I tell the story and set up encounters and stuff."

"I want to play," said Angie. She stood. "Can Moray and I play?"

Jason looked queasy, "I don't think we will all fit around the coffee table."

"We can play here," said Angie. "We have a card table."

Jason opened and closed his mouth, but no sound came out. It wouldn't have mattered anyway, whatever he would have said. We were on a path of inevitability now.

So, the card table was set up. Folding chairs unfolded. Jason opened the red duffel and started placing books on the table. He dumped out the dice, which fascinated the girls. They picked each one up asking what it was--twenty-sided, twelve-sided, and so on. He explained the basic idea of the game, that they were playing characters in a story. They could do anything a real person could do, and more, because they would have special powers and abilities. They absorbed all this without any indication of snark or judgement. Jason seemed to relax, entering his element.

Angie rolled up a Halfling thief named Haggita Baggins because she had read The Hobbit in third grade. Moray had to be the cleric, desperately needed for its healing ability. This entered her into a long and undistinguished line of tag-a-long friends, girlfriends, and little sisters who were forced to play the cleric. All told it took about an hour.

"Okay," said Jason, at last. "You guys meet in a tavern called The Wobbly Wendigo…"

***

A week or so after that first session Moray broke her ankle trying to do a trick on her older brother's skateboard, so she couldn't go to the pool, didn't want to crutch around the mall, and didn't want Angie to have any fun without her. We ended up playing a few days a week, and then almost every day.

Angie's grandpa, Merle, the one who was in WWII, would sit and watch us play. "Better than soaps," he'd say. On breaks he would show us things he got during the campaign. Nazi SS pins, a lighter with a swastika on it, plates and cutlery, even a gun he had taken from a dead Nazi outside of Berlin. It had a swastika on it, too. He couldn't stand for long and was on oxygen.

"I've often wondered how many allies and Jews this gun killed," he said when he showed it to us. It was wrapped in a white kerchief and kept in an old cigar box. He looked at it with some mixture of respect and horror. It was the only gun I had ever seen. My expression wasn't mixed at all.

As June ended and July came, so did a heat wave. Nothing is more intolerable to an Oregonian than a daily high of anything over eighty-five degrees. When it gets to ninety, people start actually dying. Ninety-nine and up is apocalypse. No one talks about anything else. The news is mostly about how hot it is, how hot is was, and how much longer it will be hot.

"It's friggin' hot," said Kyle one Saturday after the 4th.

Merle sat at the spigot next to the garage door filling water balloons at Angie's request. "Ain't even ten o'clock yet," he said.

Angie came out of the house with a pitcher of red Kool-Aid and some paper cups.

"God, it's hot out here," she said. "It's like a wall of heat."

Jason wore black pants and a short sleeve polo.

"Aren't you dying?" said Angie.

"I'm fine," he said. "In the Arab world they are covered head to toe. Protects them from the sun."

"It feels like Arabia," said Moray. She threw her arms out, "Lawrence of Arabia."

Kyle fanned himself with his character sheet.

"Can we start?" I said. I felt a ball of iron in my stomach. Angie and my characters were developing a close relationship in the game. Turns out Haggita was a victim of domestic abuse back in the village she lived in before becoming an adventurer. A few sessions ago we learned that the necromancer holed up in the Tower of Thurn was Bolo, her abusive ex. Haggita, cowered in fear of him. Angie said she read an article about abused women and their conditioned terror. Whatever, I had Paj'di fireball him. As an illusionist, I hated to use such a vulgar display of power as a rule, but as an adventuring magic user, you do need to have some utility up your sleeve. After that, Angie adored me, or Haggita adored Paj'di anyway. Angie started saying "My hero" every time I walked into the garage. To me that was just a short step from "I love you." Same syllables even.

"Overnight the snow came down even harder," began Jason, "so it was hard even to push the heavy door of the Seven Peaks Inn open in the morning. You all wrap your cloaks tighter and brace against the cold, as you trudge silently towards Fire-Drake Mountain."

"I give my cloak to Haggita," I say, nearly jumping out of my seat.

"Wait, I think I can make us warm," said Moray. She snatched up her character sheet. "Yes, right here. Resist Cold."

Of course she could.

"Indeed," said Jason. "Yarom approaches each of you in turn and touches you, and you become warm."

Kyle snorted.

"Thank you Priestess Yarom," I say.

"Her aid come none too soon, as the snow begins to fall again, in earnest. It is difficult to see, but the red glow from the mountaintop still serves as a beacon. You remember that here you will face your greatest, most deadly test yet, Gorrhorim the Ember, Guardian of the Runesword."

We are appropriately silent at the utterance of his name.

"As you clear the timberline you see the rickety suspension bridge that crosses the Black Chasm of Nothrindir."

"I pull out my sword," said Kyle.

"What for?" I said. "It's a bridge."

"I pull out my sword, I said," said Kyle.

"Test-ost-er-one," sang Angie.

Jason rolled a die behind his Dungeon Master's screen. "You hear something," he said.

"What," we all said, more or less simultaneously.

"I know that sound," said Jason. He had dropped his register to indicate it was not him, but Rand speaking. Rand was a ranger NPC (non-player character) that Jason ran in the party. I didn't really like that. It felt like cheating. "Ice spiders."

Jason flipped back to his regular voice. "From the edge of the chasm you see great chitinous legs lift up bulbous icy bodies of giant frozen spiders. They chatter as they approach you, and their legs snap and pop as they walk."

"That's why I pulled out my sword," said Kyle.

"Prepare for a fight," said Jason as Rand.

"How many are there?" I ask.

"Nine," said Jason.

"I pull out my short sword and my dagger and sneak behind Kyle," said Angie. This was not from fear, she was trying to manoeuvre behind the spiders to backstab.

"It's Stan," said Kyle.

"I'm not calling you Stan," said Angie.

"That's my character's name."

"It's a stupid D and D name," she said.

Kyle pointed at Moray, "Her name is stupid. It's just her real name backwards."

"It sounds good though," said Moray. "High Priestess Yarom." She flung her arms out like she was Lawrence of Arabia again.

"All right," said Jason, ending the argument. "Roll initiative."

We rolled and reported out our results. I got a +2 from my Amulet of Alacrity that I plucked off Bolo's still smoldering corpse.

"Paj is first," said Jason.

"Color Spray," I announce.

"Why don't you just fireball them," said Kyle.

"I'm an Illusionist."

"Why'd you have to pick the weakest magic user?"

"Shut up *Stan*," I said. Truth was I wasn't supposed to have Fireball. Jason worked it into the game that I learned it from a dying wizard because, when it was just Kyle and I, we needed something to really damage monsters. I had since learned the power of the Illusionist is not in the spells, it's in the imagination.

"Color Spray," I say again.

"A fan of dazzling colors shoots from Paj'di's fingertips and," Jason rolls behind the screen, "four of the spiders screech and fumble around blindly."

"I stab one in the eye," said Kyle.

"Not your turn yet," said Jason. "It's Haggita's."

Angie sat forward. "I dive behind the closest one and backstab it."

"Haggita rolls forward, but the spider is too quick and picks her up in its forelimbs. Then it dashes back towards the chasm with her in its icy grip."

"What?" said Angie.

"I cast Spiritual Hammer," said Moray.

"It misses," said Jason.

"Wait," I say, "you aren't rolling for any of this."

"Is it my turn yet?" said Kyle.

"This isn't fair," protested Angie.

"As the spider nears the rim of the chasm, Rand leaps into action, sprinting towards Haggita and her captor."

"Oh jeeze," said Moray, flopping back and crossing her arms.

Jason ignored her. "As he sprints he readies his bow and notches an arrow. He has one chance. The blinded spiders thrash about and get in the way of his shot. He continues his course, though, and using one as a springboard leaps into the air, firing the arrow."

"Is it my turn?" said Kyle. "That was like five turns."

"The arrow pierces the back of the spiders thorax and lodges in its brain, killing it instantly. The spider's limbs contract and it hits the icy ground, releasing Haggita. Both now are sliding towards the edge of the chasm. Right before Haggita goes over, falling to certain death, Rand catches her by the ankle."

"This is bullshit," I said, finding myself on my feet. Things were coming together. I felt like I was seeing everything clear, all at once.

"I love you," said Jason, "says Rand."

"What?" both girls said.

"What about the spiders," said Kyle.

"I know that you are a halfling, and that I am a man. We are different, but that doesn't matter. Love will bridge that chasm. And then Rand lifts her to into his arms and they kiss."

"No they don't," said Angie. "I didn't-"

I interrupted. "I cast Spectral Force. The illusion is that a spider crawls out of the chasm and grabs Rand, dragging him into the abyss."

"I disbelieve," said Jason.

"Why? You wouldn't have any reason to," I said.

"Well, we have to roll to see if you hit." He moved his hand behind the screen.

"I'll do it," I said. Jason usually rolled everything. He said it kept up the suspension of disbelief and made things flow better. We figured he fudged rolls now and again. Plus, I was the only one who had a set of dice besides him. I brought them each session and fiddled with them in slow moments. I picked up the 20 sided and chucked it into the middle of the table.

Natural 20.

"You're dead," I said.

"That was cool," said Kyle. We high-fived.

"I- you can't just-" Jason struggled, but he couldn't escape the absolute power of the roll. If the game is life, the dice are God.

"God don't lie," I said.

He was still for a moment, and in that moment my triumph twisted into remorse. It was the look he had on his face. He looked like, well, *sadness*.

"She comes with me," he said at last. "I was holding her, so we go together. We both go over the edge into the darkness."

"Bullshit," said Angie.

"Watch your language, young lady," said Merle, who was still by the spigot, but was smoking a pipe now.

Everyone was standing now, except Kyle. Moray balanced on one leg.

From the street a squeal of tires broke the spell. A tan Honda Accord jumped the sidewalk and rammed into Angie's mailbox, which was brick and looked like a chimney except with a mailbox in it. It was Jason's mother's car. After a long pause where no one seemed to move, she fell out of the car. Her forehead, bleeding.

"I'm so sorry," she said to Merle. "I'm so sorry. Oh fuck, look at my car. I'm so- oh, who's blood is this." She reached into her purse and took out a pint of Wild Turkey, unscrewed it, and took a few pulls. "Goddamn," she said.

Jason didn't move. If you could be dead and still standing up that's what he looked like. Nothing registered on his face, or in the way his chest moved, or anything. No rage, no sadness, no shame--just nothing. No one looked at him but me. They all watched his mother wobble around the driveway.

"Kathy, you hit your head when you crashed, I think," said Merle.

She touched her forehead and then looked at her fingers. "I'm bleeding," she said.

"I think we ought to call an ambulance," said Merle.

"What? Over this?" said Kathy, opening her purse. "Oh, this is nothing. I've had way worse. Just a little ice and a little more medicine, right?" She took a compact from her purse. Blood was really running from her forehead now. It was tough to tell how big the cut was. "Jason, come to mommy and help me into the house. Chop-chop."

Jason still didn't move.

Kathy opened the compact and looked into it, lowering her chin and looking over the top of these big sunglasses she had on. She was in a white sleeveless dress and had on pink jellies, like the girls at school wore, and those big, round sunglasses. She looked all mixed up.

"Oh, shit," she said, and then her knees gave way.

"I think we ought to call an ambulance," said Merle again.

Things got weird after that.

***

By the time the cops got there that day something fundamental had changed in my life. I felt it at the time, but didn't have any real idea of what was happening. It was the first bad thing. Before that, there were few bad things, none really. After that it was like all the bad things were falling through the door that one bad thing had opened, and were piling up on each other.

Kathy was taken to the hospital by the EMTs and then to the county lock-up by the cops. Jason rode with her in the ambulance, robotically climbing into the back without saying anything to, or even looking at, the rest of us. I packed his books and things into his red bag, slung it over my shoulder, and took it home. I watched from my front porch, waiting for him to come back so I could give him his stuff. The afternoon faded. Angie was in her garage, alone. When the street lights came on she got up, turned on the overhead light, and sat back in her big clam-shell chair.

At around ten-thirty, a cop car showed up. The cop and Jason got out and went inside his house. A bit later the came back to the car and Jason threw a bag into the trunk. I took his red bag up and started walking that direction. At about the same time, Angie crossed her driveway and started talking to Jason. I got to the middle of the street, where I could sorta hear them, and stopped. Angie cupped her hands over her mouth and nose. She shook her head slightly.

"I'm sorry," she kept saying. Then Jason spoke, but I couldn't make it out and she said she was sorry again.

Jason did something strange then. He reached up and gently moved her hands from her face. That was it. I walked backwards, watching them stand there. I backed all the way to our side yard. Jason turned, finally, and got into the cop car, and the cop drove them off. Angie watched the car go down the street, went into the garage, and turned off the light. I could hear the motor of the garage door as it lurched shut, finishing with a solid *whump*.

And that was it.

***

I spent the next few weeks of the summer playing with JPJ, for the most part. Kyle went off to Bible Camp, Jason was MIA, and Angie' garage door had been closed. I did see Moray, her cast off, walking around the block. We just waved. I tried to play *D&D* with JPJ, but playing with just a DM and one PC wasn't as cool as a full party. We spent some time melting and burying *Star Wars* figures (his, no way I'd melt mine) and playing *Tunnel Runner* on my Atari. His mother bought him a nudie mag, which seemed really weird to me, but it mostly had boobs in it and even an article on breastfeeding. We crawled into the recycle drops and found real *Playboys*, which were way different from the other magazine.

One morning in early August I was on my way to JPJ's and I saw cop cars again in front of Angie's house. Her garage door was open and she stood with Merle and Jason, talking to the officers. I forgot all about JPJ and headed over.

"...a box of plates from Berlin." Merle was talking to the officers. "They have swastikas on the bottom. There was a box of pins and medals from SS officers. Iron Crosses and like that. Out of all of it it's the box of photos I want back. Oh, and the pistol."

The cop writing looked up. "There was a firearm?" he said.

"Yeah, a Luger. Had the SS symbol on the grip," said Merle.

"Is it functional?" said the cop who didn't hold a clipboard.

"Yessir," said Merle. "Hasn't been fired in forty years though."

The cops looked at each other. The one without the clipboard went to the car and got on the radio.

The other cop turned to Jason. "You say you saw them?"

"What happened? What's going on?" I say.

Angie looked like she had been crying. "Someone broke into the garage and stole a bunch of Grandpa's war stuff."

My stomach sank. I'm not sure why. I hadn't heard of anyone's house getting broken into before.

"I did," said Jason. "I was in the back yard. You can see their side door into the garage from there."

"And you saw them," said Clipboard.

"Yes."

"What were they doing?"

"What do you mean?" said Jason. "They were stealing stuff. Boxes, what they could carry."

"What'd they look like?"

Jason didn't hesitate. "Like black kids. I mean, they were black kids. Three of them. They had on red hoodies. Probably Crips from downtown, looking for crack money. Scoundrels."

"Bloods," said Clipboard.

"What," said Jason.

"Bloods wear red. Crips wear blue," said Clipboard.

Jason scowled for a split second. "I know, I just-
Well, I yelled at them. I said 'Hey, what do you guys
think you're doing? I'm calling the cops.' And then
they ran up the street."

"Which way," said Clipboard. Jason nodded the
direction.

"They pointed a gun at me, or I would have made
chase."

"Made chase, huh?" said Clipboard.

Merle interrupted. "What's this world comin' to? We
got gang members comin' out here to rob us to buy
crack. I see on the news what the city's like. What
are you boys doin' about it?"

Clipboard opened his mouth like he was going to
speak and then turned and walked to the car.

"That's what I thought," said Merle. He went into
the garage and started shifting things around,
muttering to himself.

Jason took one step towards Angie. "I can find them," he said. "I saw them, and I know how to find them."

"No," said Angie.

Jason put his fist into his palm as he talked. "Cops are dumb. They won't know I'm looking for them. I'll just look like another guy."

"No," said Angie.

"I can help," I said. I think they forgot I was there.

"Oh, Sam," said Angie. "You are such a good kid."

Kid. That one stung.

"Jason," I said. "I have your bag. Your books."

"What?" said Jason.

The cop who was on the radio came back. He looked down at me. "Who are you?" he said.

"I'm Sam. I live over there," I said.

"You see anything going on over here this morning?" he said.

"No," I said.

"Then why don't you run along."

"Okay," I said. "I just was worried."

"Thanks, Sam," said Angie. She sorta leaned over when she said this, to get eye to eye.

I hopped on my bike and headed to JPJ's.

***

That was the last time I saw Jason. I happened to be thinking about it on Kyle's couch one afternoon while he took his turn on *Super Mario Bros. 2*. We found a copy to rent at a video store in Clackamas. You couldn't find it in the stores because of the chip shortage. He played Luigi, mostly, and I played Toad. We took turns. Of course, I didn't know it was the last time I was going to see him as I sat there, but, at that point, it had been nearly a month. A 'For Sale' sign went up in his yard. I wanted to ask Angie what was going on, but she had left to be a counsellor at some summer camp a few days after the robbery.

At any rate, I was thinking about it that afternoon. Kyle's mom was on the phone in the kitchen with her toes on the counter, painting them.

"...met his mother at a meeting. I mean, people there are wrecks, right, by definition. But this gal, well, I think she was into some of the harder stuff. That was the sense I got from the way she was acting. Real twitchy, that gal. She acted like she didn't know I lived right down the street from her. She was trying to, like, ignore me. Probably embarrassed, like the neighborhood thought she was a model citizen or something. Like she's Nancy Reagan, or something."

I leaned over the arm of the couch so I could hear better, everything looked upside down.

"Right. So, she comes up to me at the coffee station at the end of the meeting. She says hello and then asks how long I've been going. I said three years sober. Wow, she says. Wow, only three days here, she says. I give her a smile. I said I think our boys are friends. They play that dragon game together, I say."

"Then she starts in about this kid. He's in juvie. He stole a gun from the neighbor's garage. Some kind of Nazi gun. And some other stuff. All this Nazi stuff the old guy over there brought back from the war."

"I know. But you wanna know the weird part. He brought the gun back. Like, for a day or two he was the hero. He told them he went down into Chinatown and found the robbers. Black kids, he said. Can you imagine? Chinatown, for crying-out-loud. Like he's Jack Nicholson, or something."

She chuckled at this.

"Well, they found out a few days later it was him all along. He tried to pawn some Nazi dishes. Well, the cops had contacted all the pawn shops in the area, just in case, and sure enough, he shows up with a box of Nazi plates. He was headed to foster care, you know, permanently. His mom said he planned on using the money from the plates to move to London. Can you believe that? London."

She paused. I could hear the other lady on the phone, but just murmurs.

"I don't know. Maybe he thought the gun would attract too much attention at a shop. I mean, he's not the smartest bulb on the tree, right? I mean, I guess he could have sold it on the street."

She paused again. Murmuring.

"Well, no, that's the point. He didn't *actually* go get the stuff from black kids in Chinatown. It was all made up. The boy was the one who stole the stuff."

Pause.

"I can't say I know. His mother hadn't even talked to him. She's a mess remember. She lost him. He's in foster care. I think he's better off, Janey. I mean it. That woman is a nut-job."

"But yeah," she said at last. "I have no idea why a kid would do something like that."

***

The next day my parent got divorced. I felt like I was underwater. I stayed in my room for a week, at first just staring at the ceiling, but soon I had opened the red bag and started reading the books. It was different from when I tried to learn to play before. I had a teacher. Jason's handwriting decorated the margins. Light pencil, slanted, condensing information, cross-referencing, even house rules. It was like he was there with me.

My plan was to launch a campaign as Dungeon Master. I would bring the party back together. I thought of Angie. This was something to hope for.

Merle died in September. Heart attack. They had an open house after the funeral. My dad bought me a button up and a tie and took me over. There were tables of baked goods--cookies, cupcakes, rice krispie treats, pies, muffins. You could eat however much you wanted, too. No one was paying attention. It would have been awesome if it wasn't for all the sadness.

Angie stood next to the peanut butter bars. I went up to her. I wasn't sure what to say. I said I had a campaign. I showed her my house key on the shoelace around my neck. She started crying. She cried so hard I just sort of drifted away.

I started the campaign, though. Kyle and JPJ, and then we recruited the Ford brothers from up the hill. Their parents were hardcore Bible types and forbid them from playing *D&D*, which is why I think they liked it so much. This other kid started showing up, too, Paul. He saw me with the DMG at in math class. I was his friend at that moment whether I liked it or not. Paul was a strange one. He wore Coke-bottles and didn't seem to bend his legs when he walked.

We played every day. I don't think there was a kid in the neighborhood who didn't play with us at least once. My dad didn't get it, but he bought me books. It wasn't long before I had quite a collection, including *Fiend Folio*, and *Deities and Demigods*. Truth was, with him at work, I could have been doing much worse.

Angie smiles when she sees me. She seems older now. I think she has a boyfriend, but that really doesn't bother me. I was too busy for a girlfriend, anyway, with all the game prep. Sometimes, though, when I'm on my porch and she is in her garage, in her clamshell, I linger, and try to make it seem like I'm not looking.

———

Dan Coffey is an English Literature teacher from Portland, Oregon. 'The Illusionist' is his first story in print.

Finding Home

by Paula Dempsey

Things smelt strange. Xian had been aware of the big crate for some weeks now. It appeared for a time every day, then disappeared again. Today it was sitting there, in his enclosure. It smelt funny but it wasn't scary. The human who fed him arrived with it every day then gave Xian a treat. The human who fed him wouldn't let anything scary near him so Xian felt safe.

Today there were other humans there too. There was the woman who smelt funny and sometimes stuck things in Xian which hurt. And there were humans who were new; he hadn't smelt them before. The human who fed Xian opened a window in the crate and Xian went in to investigate. The crate was full of soft bedding and there was bamboo to eat. He sat down and took a bite. The window quickly closed. Xian could hear voices then the crate moved, smoothly going upwards then gently bumping down. It was dark and Xian could smell that he wasn't in his enclosure any more. The human who fed him was there, so Xian told himself he was safe. He ate some more bamboo as the box started to move again.

***

On a cold day in February Melissa pedalled her bicycle along a city street, past the grocery store and the gas station, dodging the delivery trucks and the buses, on her way to the community centre, where every Wednesday evening she met up with some friends to play board games. They weren't close friends; she didn't see them any other time. They didn't text each other or email. They just met up every Wednesday, laughed, ate pizza and played board games.

The community centre was a square, one storey red brick building with a tin roof. Broken paving stones formed a small parking lot in front of the door. The other three sides were overgrown with weeds. The whole area was enclosed by a chain link fence. There was no gate, just a jagged gap in the fence. A road ran in front of the building. The community centre was surrounded on the other three sides by apartment blocks made of concrete. Since the graffiti had been removed, there was no colour.

***

The gentle bumping of the crate made Xian sleepy. The journey passed quickly, as he napped then ate more bamboo. Then he was still, and there were different voices. He could see through the window as more humans came to put his crate onto a big thing. The human who fed him stayed with him and lots of people were talking and pointing at Xian. Xian knew that he was important but he wanted to know where he was going. He drank some water as the doors of the big thing closed and it went dark again. There was a roaring, whining noise, then his body felt heavier and the bumping got worse. Xian wished he could see out. And he wished his ears would stop popping.

***

"So explain, what is Takenoko?"

Rodney's voice was muffled as he unpacked the box.

"It's a game set in the garden of the Japanese emperor. And he has a panda..."

"Excuse me, pandas do not live in Japan," said Amanda, the slightly annoying woman who always argued about rules. Sally frowned at the interruption.

"I was about to explain," Rodney went on patiently. "The Japanese emperor has received the panda as a gift from the emperor of China, and he's asked his gardener to grow some bamboo to feed the panda."

Rodney ran through the rules. Takenoko was played, and everyone had a good time. People laughed, the pizza was good. It was 10pm and Melissa got back on her bicycle, looking around carefully before slowly pedalling back onto the main road, and, picking up speed, heading for home.

Sally also lived across town, in a squat with some other artists. As she boarded the subway she thought about the portrait she was working on at the moment, a painting of a homeless man who sat outside the station near her home. She hoped she'd caught his character. She'd check in daylight tomorrow, maybe make a few changes.

Amanda didn't have so far to travel. She lived in an apartment in one of the blocks behind the community centre with her mother who was ninety three. Amanda loved her mother very much, but she liked playing games for a few hours each week. It was her time and now it was over. She settled her mother into bed then made herself some hot milk. She thought about the game of Takenoko. Was it quite right that Rodney had got the green bamboo in the last round? Maybe it was. Then her mother called. Amanda fetched her a glass of water, then went to bed herself.

***

Rodney locked up the Community Centre, as he did every Wednesday. He dropped the key through the janitor's letterbox and went to his own apartment in the block across from Amanda's. He made himself coffee in the tiny kitchen and switched on his laptop. He glanced at the photo of his daughter who lived with her mother across town. Although traffic roared by on the highway, Rodney's place always felt kind of quiet.

***

Xian was feeling bored. He'd been in the box for a long time and he'd almost finished his food. The human who fed him gave him fresh water. He felt his ears pop again then a sudden whooshing sensation and a big bump. He was moving very quickly. Then there was daylight and more voices. Xian saw a lot of people. They were making that sort of noise that humans make when they are happy. Xian thought the people were happy to see him and he felt proud. He knew he was a very special panda.

The crate moved again and this time Xian could look out. The humans looked blurry because he was moving so quickly. It felt like a long time before everything stopped. When it did, Xian looked out. He could see his new home. It was big and had lots of bushes and places to hide and a pool.

***

The following week a young woman appeared at the board games group for the first time. She was small and slender with pale skin, a turned up nose and black hair pulled back from her face. She wore a big yellow fluffy sweater and brown yoga pants. She looked like a little bird.

Amanda introduced her.

"This is Zinnia, my new neighbour. She'd like to play Takenoko"

Zinnia smiled nervously. "Amanda says you have this great game about pandas. I love pandas." She blushed and blinked around the room.

"Hi Zinnia. Come and join us." Rodney was always kind to new people. Sally went to another table to play something else while Melissa and Amanda and Rodney and Zinnia played Takenoko. And they laughed, and they got mushrooms on the pizza because Zinnia liked mushrooms.

When the evening ended Zinnia went back to her apartment on the top floor of the block. It was small, but Zinnia had done her best to make it nice. There were shelves for her books and lots of photos in frames on the walls. Photography gave her a sense of connection to the city as she documented its daily activity; people in the streets, cats on walls, flowers in the park. Sometimes people chatted to her when she asked permission to take their pictures and that made her happy.

***

Zinnia was excited that a panda had arrived at the zoo. She went as often as she could. Sometimes she took photos. She talked to the panda, until somebody said she was being weird. That was a shame, because the panda seemed to enjoy the conversation, although it was a little one-sided.

So Zinnia went to the zoo early in the morning, before the crowds. She often talked to the panda then. She told him stories about China, where he was from. She just asked him how he was doing. It didn't really matter what she talked about, the panda seemed to enjoy it.

***

It was April and the city was waking up. Flowers appeared in window boxes, cats sunbathed on balconies. Melissa arrived at the community centre early one Wednesday, and met Zinnia outside.

"I was thinking, it's a shame that the community centre looks so dull" said Zinnia.

Melissa looked around and agreed.

Amanda arrived, then Rodney with the key, then Sally. And the evening progressed as usual.

By the following Wednesday the tallest weeds had been cut down and part of the overgrown ground had been dug up. Sally suggested this might be the work of Community Association but Amanda said she was on the committee and would have been told of any planned work.

The next week Melissa saw that the whole area had been dug over and it looked like someone had made a bonfire of the weeds. A hexagonal patch of bare soil had been created, surrounded by broken concrete that was too hard to dig. Amanda admitted that everything looked very tidy but she wasn't sure that someone should have done anything without permission. Sally said she didn't care about permission because the patch looked like someone was taking care of it and that had to be good, right?

Zinnia smiled, and Amanda saw that smile. "Was this you?" she asked, aggressively. "I know you're new, but there are rules. This isn't your private land, you know. You can't just do things without asking the Community Association first!"

Zinnia looked like she was about to cry. Sally said quietly "Zinnia has done something positive, Amanda."

Amanda didn't say anything else, but she did leave Zinnia alone.

When Melissa arrived the next week, Zinnia and Sally were both in the garden. "I'm helping!" called Sally. "Look, we have some bamboo! Zinnia's put it where there's lots of sunshine!" And some people noticed for the very first time that the sun did shine on the grey apartment blocks, and the red community centre.

Melissa looked thoughtful. "Bamboo needs lots of water. Perhaps I can help with that." And a few days later a large package was delivered to Zinnia's flat. The box said Rainwater Irrigation System. Zinnia smiled with delight and baked some cookies for the games group as a thank you to Melissa.

***

Xian looked forward to his visits from the human creature that smelt different. She made a lot of noises that he couldn't understand, but she didn't seem like a threat. It would have been nicer if she'd brought food. Sometimes she held up a box-thing in front of her face. A lot of the humans did that. Sometimes the box-thing flashed, which Xian didn't like. Then the humans would look at the box-thing and make happy noises. Xian didn't understand that either. He got bored with it and went to hide. Then the people made different noises.

***

By May there were lots of neighbours helping Zinnia make the garden. One elderly woman brought a lavender bush which she said reminded her of the fields she played in when she was a little girl. A man dug a hole for some sunflower seeds and hoped they would add a splash of yellow to the wall of the community centre. Sally contributed some ivy which she planned to train around the chain link fence to hide the cold, dull metal. A small boy planted an orange pip which might become a tree one day. Not everything would work, but everyone was welcome to try.

Rodney wasn't good at gardening, but he found a couple of old chairs in a dumpster and painted them pale blue. He put them in the garden with an upturned crate for a table and he didn't mind when Amanda said it looked messy.

Zinnia was most proud of the bamboo she'd planted, right by the gap in the fence so you had to walk past it on the way in. Zinnia and Rodney spent a lot of time together in the garden, using Melissa's present to water the bamboo. Zinnia showed Rodney how to dig the ground and put in plants, then they would sit on the old chairs, drink beer and talk.

***

Zinnia showed her panda photos to the board games group. Amanda said they were there to play games not look at photos. Melissa said it would only take a moment and the photos were really good. Zinnia was a bit upset that Amanda didn't like the photos and apologised a lot.

Melissa didn't cycle home straight away that evening. She waited until everyone had gone except Rodney who, as usual, was locking up the community centre.

***

The next Wednesday, Rodney did something really brave. He asked Zinnia if he could go with her to see the panda next Saturday. Zinnia did something really brave too. She said yes.

Melissa and Sally worked in the garden while Zinnia and Rodney were at the zoo. Amanda had to look after her mother but she came down from time to time with coffee and checked that nothing was happening that the Community Association didn't like.

Rodney and Zinnia stayed at the zoo for a long time. They visited Xian, the panda. Then they saw the lions and the tigers, the fish and the snakes, even the antelopes who were a bit boring. They ate ice cream then they went to see Xian again. Xian seemed pleased to see Zinnia.

When the zoo closed, they caught the subway back to their apartments. As they got to the garden Zinnia gave a tiny squeak then put her hands over her mouth. On the bare brick wall, near the gap in the fence, was a perfect portrait of Xian, right behind Zinnia's bamboo. It had been painted by Sally, with Melissa's help.

"To say thank you for making our garden," Sally said. Lots of people were out in the garden in the sunshine and everyone clapped. Even Amanda was smiling.

Zinnia didn't go to the zoo so often after that. She was busy with the garden and she spent a lot of time with Rodney. She had the photographs and Sally's painting to remind her of Xian. Xian didn't miss her that much. He was a panda. He had his own business to take care of.

———

Paula Dempsey is a London-based writer for role-playing games including Trail of Cthulhu, Call of Cthulhu, Urban Shadows and Malandros. Her latest book, The Book of the New Jerusalem (for Trail of Cthulhu) will be published in 2018.

A Meeple's Tale
by David Mitchell

"It's you! Oh, thank the powers! I am so pleased to see you!"

"Who said that? Oh, hi kid. Are you okay?"

"Much better now you're here. I was so scared."

"Yeah, well, you're safe now. Don't worry, kid."

"Great! Thank you, so much. I should say though, I'm not really a kid."

"You sure look like a kid."

"I'm a lot older than I look."

"So if you aren't a kid, what are you?"

"Well, it's difficult to say. I have been many things - a knight, a farmer, a highwayman... that's my earliest memory, actually, being a highwayman."

"A highwayman? You? You robbed people?"

"Sure did. Stand and deliver! Ha ha."

"Did you have a horse?"

"Yes, of course... at least I think I did. I must have had one, surely... I can't actually remember what it looked like though. It was a long time ago."

"But you're just a kid."

"I told you, I'm not a kid. Or at least, I wasn't back then, in my armed robbery days."

"You're not making any sense, kid."

"It's confusing, I know. There were lots of other things that made no sense either."

"Like what?"

"Well, for example, the road that I operated on, my patch, was one that did not actually lead anywhere."

"Why would such a road exist?"

"That's what I thought! I don't know. Eventually, though, a town did appear at one end of the road, and then they built a monastery at the other end. For some reason, at that point, I decided to give up being a highwayman, and became the chief abbot at the monastery instead.

"Maybe you wanted to atone for your sins?"

"It wasn't up to me though. It was the powers that be."

"The what?"

"The powers that be. I hear their voices all the time."

"What do they say?"

"They tell me who I am, and what to do."

"So what did they tell you to do when you were the abbot?"

"They told me to expand the monastery grounds - to acquire all the land around the building."

"And did you?"

"Yes. I worked so hard - preaching, fundraising, and appealing to all the local lords and ladies, telling everyone that I was on a mission from the powers that be, to surround the monastery with fields and roads and cities. And we did it! I remember the sense of pride I felt when we built the final section of road just behind the monastery; and I sensed that the powers that be were really pleased."

"So then what happened?"

"I lost my job."

"That doesn't sound fair."

"No, but it's okay, I became a knight. I defended a city, while it was under construction."

"That sounds pretty cool."

"I guess. But a complaint was made against me by a princess, and I had to leave. I went back to being a highwayman again, and then I got eaten by a dragon."

"Well that sucks."

"It sure does. Being eaten didn't do much long-term harm though, and I went off and joined the circus. I was on the bottom row of a human pyramid for a short while, but that did not last long either. It sure was a confusing time - I kept changing my job all the time, just as it was getting interesting. The only job I could ever seem to hold down for any length of time was being a farmer. That was hard work - I always seemed to be on my hands and knees, digging ... or something ... it's a bit of a blur to be honest. I think there might have been a pig at one point."

"This all sounds a bit ... unlikely."

"Things got even more confusing after that. I started to hear the voices of the powers that be saying a phrase I had never heard before."

"What phrase?"

"*Spare meeple.* They said I was a spare meeple. I had no idea what that meant, but it was after I started hearing that, that I kept waking up in places I did not recognise at all. Really weird places."

"What sort of weird places?"

"I woke up in a village, with a number 4 written on stickers on my chest and back. I was very upset."

"Because you're not a number, you're a free man? Heh heh. Right?"

"What?"

"Were you a prisoner? Heh heh."

"Why is that funny?"

"Never mind."

"I went back to one of my old professions, and joined the church. For some reason I spent a lot of time in a cotton bag."

"Heh heh. You were a man of the cloth."

"Oh yes. I get that one. Very funny. Anyway, I eventually came out of the bag, and then the powers that be decided I should go and stand on the window ledge instead."

"That's er ... unusual."

"It was as nice window."

"Well, that's something."

"Just as my career was taking off though, they made me go and lie on my back, on a massive book, for what seemed like eternity."

111

"Sounds uncomfortable."

"I travelled a lot after that - Glen More… Troyes… The Sultanate of Naqala. I also spent some time in a place called Meeple City, but I didn't like it there - it was terrifying. Monsters kept attacking, and instead of running away, everyone just stood around, holding up the ceilings of multi-storey carparks. I was glad to leave that place, I can tell you."

"Then what?"

"I went on a big wooden ship, to the new world. The powers that be told me that they wanted to acquire some land there. So me and two other guys went to an auction to get it for them. There were a couple of other bidders interested in it too, but we got it because, if I understood correctly, there were more of us. After acquiring the land though, instead of me going to work on it, the powers decided it would be best if I spent some time inside another big cloth bag instead."

"Another one? What is it with you and bags."

"Dunno. Sometimes I woke up in interesting places though. One time I found myself in a tiny western. It was epic. I played poker. I did feel a bit self-conscious though, as I was the only one there without a hat."

"A man needs a hat."

"Another time I was in this land called Terran Mystical, or something like that. There, I was ... er ... I was ... hmmm ..."

"You were what?"

"I don't really know, to be honest. It was a very complicated place, and most of the time I did not really know what was going on."

"Heavy."

"Yes. Then, for several years, I was living in the stone age."

"In what way?"

"In the literal way. I travelled through time to get to the stone age. The powers that be made me part of a tribe. We went hunting, we collected wood, we built an abacus. Sometimes we even found gold in the river. I had a huge bar of gold once, but we had to trade it for some berries, because we forgot to go hunting."

"That doesn't sound like a good deal."

"That's what I said, but it wasn't up to me."

"The powers that be?"

"Yep."

"Are you winding me up, kid?"

113

"No, I promise. It's all true."

"You've led a strange life."

"I have led many strange lives."

"So how long have you been here, hiding in this grocery store?"

"I don't know. It's hard to keep track of time."

"And what do the voices in your head tell you that you are now?"

"It's a strange thing - it's a phrase I have never heard before."

"What phrase?"

"Helpless survivor."

"Heh heh! Well kid, to be honest, you do kinda look helpless."

"Can we go to your home now, please? The one at the North Pole."

"The North Pole? … oh … yeah ...heh ... the North Pole. Sure, why not?

Only, normally, we just call it The Compound."

"Thanks Santa!"

"Heh heh. No problem. Better put on a coat though, kid - it's the dead of winter out there."

———

David Mitchell is not <u>the</u> David Mitchell. He is not even the <u>other</u> David Mitchell. He is, however, <u>a</u> David Mitchell, and nobody can that that away from him.

Legacy

by P.E. Pryce

The Gothenburg Mega-Sprawl, 2042

"Why did you betray me, Erik?"

The young man did not answer his superior, and once again, the room fell silent.

Rain pattered against the polycarbonate windows of the high rise building. They were high up, in the executive offices, and if Erik had dared lift his eyes from the floor, he would have seen the dark storm clouds that descended over the sprawling metropolis like vultures at the feed.

"Why did you betray me, Erik?" the man repeated. His words were clipped and precise, and his tone hinted at a hideous fury that lay beneath. It was the voice of power absolute, a voice that made Erik tremble even more.

Still, he said nothing.

The man sighed audibly. He whipped up his hands up and slammed them down onto the table with force. Game pieces scattered to the ground. Instinctively, Erik fell to his knees.

No, No, No! That was my chance. My salvation!

Erik scurried under the table. One by one, his quivering hands placed the pieces back on the board where he thought they had been. He blinked back tears. Broken.

His master slowly rose to his feet. Two of his bodyguards stepped forwards, ready to aid him out of his chair if needed. The man furrowed his already wrinkled brow and they stepped aside. He brushed the merest hint of dust from his shoulders.

Lightning chose this moment to strike. It slashed wickedly across the sky in the distance, illuminating the densely packed cityscape below. The man gave Erik a long, hard stare. A shadow of a smile crossed his face, as if this terrible storm was his doing.

"You have not touched those pieces all evening, Erik," he said as a matter of fact. "I have waited patiently for you to take your move, and I have waited patiently for an explanation of your betrayal."

Erik, still placing pieces on the board, said nothing.

The man sucked his teeth and grimaced as though he tasted something foul. He clasped his hands together behind his back and nodded at the guard on his right. The guard diligently pulled a pistol from a holster at his side.

"Your silence condemns you."

Erik lifted his eyes for an instant. He saw the flash of the shot, bright against the night sky. Then nothing.

***

To Lilia's surprise, the knock at her door was quietly polite, as was the voice that followed.

"Ms Volkov? It is your turn. Mr Vasiliev is expecting you."

Lilia rolled her neck on her shoulders with a creak and a click. She swung her legs off the small cot and sat with her hands clasped, staring intently at the door. She felt old today, which was unusual, even though she supposed she was indeed old. She allowed herself a moment, closed her eyes and coaxed a small smile from her lips.

"Of course he is. I am the only one left," she replied. Her voice was soft and calm, and Lilia imagined that the guard who had come to collect her was probably straining against the door to hear. "I have been here quite a while - I hope Marin has not forgotten that I am an old woman. Those stairs will take some time."

The guard was undeterred. "Then we should go sooner rather than later if you are to be on time."

Lilia nodded to herself and rose to her feet. Her body was sore, always sore, but the cot made her aches even worse. *That wretched cot.* She pressed her fingers into her muscles to massage the pain away, hissing through her teeth whenever she got to a particularly tender spot. She went at her own pace, and eventually the guard knocked again.

"He is waiting, Ms Volkov."

Lilia moved to the door and rapped twice on it. It opened quickly. The escort hid his lack of patience poorly. His hands were on his hips rather than on the guns at his side. Lilia's keen eye glimpsed two exits just behind him.

If I were even five years younger I would have risked it.

Instead, she moved alongside him and offered up her arm.

"To Marin, then."

That rain is loud.

It was a strange first thought for Lilia to have as she entered Marin's office. There had been no windows in her room, no way to pass the time or tell the weather. Just darkness and silence. *Marin*, however, had windows from floor to ceiling- an entire wall of them he could use to gaze triumphantly over the landscape.

Lilia's room had been especially cramped as well, at least to begin with. Her now empty room was once occupied by four people, including herself. They had all been escorted to 'meetings' with Marin, and none of them had returned.

As always, her instincts told her to stay on guard.

Marin faced the storm outside, his hands clasped together behind his back. She was all the way across the room from him, but even from the doorway she picked up the scent of his aftershave. The hit of citrus and leather shook the webs from her senses and prompted her to survey the room before her meeting commenced.

There were three guards already in the room- four, if she included her escort. He was still holding her arm like a faithful son supporting his frail mother. She leaned on him more, accentuating her weariness. Each one of them had a pistol or two holstered at their sides. The one nearest Marin had something extra strapped to his back. *A sword.*

Katana.

Lilia's steps grew smaller.

Marin turned to look at her. He narrowed his eyes and watched her carefully. She knew the look well. He had seen her enter, and he had judged her to be a threat. The other two were near a huge table in the centre of the room. It was oak - *real* oak, she remembered - a rarity nowadays. One of the guards had a chamois cloth to hand, and was in the process of diligently polishing it to shining perfection.

The second kept picking up little trinkets from a board on the table. Lilia's escort took her closer and offered her a seat. She quickly realised that he wasn't picking up trinkets. Rather, game pieces from a board. *His* cloth, she noted, was stained a rusty red.

Lilia settled into her seat with trepidation. She leaned in closer to inspect the board.

A wave of recognition washed over her, and she smiled.

The company they had set up together had been one of transport and logistics, and the game that sat before them had *initially* been a pseudo corporate experiment, designed to encourage players to 'think outside the box' when it came to planning their shipping solutions. Over time, as the trends in corporate team bonding changed, they found new ways to do this. However, the board of directors still found that they played just as much of the game purely for fun, if not more.

After an undetermined time in confinement, Lilia looked at the game with a mixture of delight and disgust.

"An interesting choice, Marin."

Marin did not respond for a time. He had turned again to stare out into the storm. When he did speak, it was with a curious tilt of the head, as if he hadn't quite heard her. Lilia decided to push her luck.

"I thought overlords were supposed to play Chess 2," she said, her words painted with the thinnest coat of derision. "You have the timer for it, after all," she continued, pointing towards a small chess clock on the edge of the table. The guards exchanged sideways glances. Lilia leaned back on her chair a little and smiled. She knew they were wondering how she could get away with talking to the boss like that.

Time. Time and wisdom.

Marin clenched his fists behind his back, and Lilia knew it was time to bite her tongue. Slowly, he shuffled around to face her. He tilted his head again, and smiled. Lilia had seen that smile before, but never aimed towards her.

The shark inspecting its prey.

It had always scared her.

She suddenly felt very small. Lilia let out a deep breath as the temperature in the room seemed to rise a few degrees. Marin fixed his eyes on hers, and moved towards his seat. He waited patiently for his entourage to pull the seat out for him, then took the position opposite her. He leaned in close, and Lilia fought the urge to lean away.

Marin waited.

Lilia slowly retreated back into her seat.

Marin unfurled his right hand. Between two fingers, he held up a small, silver train carriage. "What does this remind you of, Lilia?"

It wasn't supposed to be an easy question. *He is looking for something. Something deeper.* Marin Vasiliev never wasted oxygen asking questions that he knew the answer to.

"Simpler times."

After what she assumed was weeks, maybe even months locked in that darkened room, she had been dragged before the boss and placed in front of a board- *the* board from his most treasured game. She would be expected to play, no doubt, like they had done so many times before. Yet Lilia suspected the stakes were a lot higher than any before.

She wasn't sure whether she was up to it. She just wanted to go home.

Where everything is simpler.

Marin sniffed hard and placed the carriage down carefully on the table. "Hmm," he said, almost thoughtfully. He leaned back and pursed his fingers together. The two men either side of him whisked into the foreground and started distributing the rest of the pieces. His were silver, Lilia noticed. Hers were bronze. With the pieces laid out, they dealt out the cards next, placing five of them face up for the pair of them to see.

"We are *actually* doing this, Marin? With *these-*" she pointed at the array of silver and bronze. They were using his custom board as well; it was beautifully crafted, with the details of each of Marin's *special* trade routes etched into the board. It would have taken pride and place above the mantle of any wealthy businessman, or perhaps a Head of State.

"These are antiques, Marin. They belong in your collection."

Even as she expressed her disbelief, she knew Marin was serious. He assessed the cards he had been dealt carefully, pondering which routes he would ultimately take. Lilia knew the board well, and the strategy was always the same.

All roads lead to Gothenburg. Or rather, tracks.

"Games are meant to be played, Lilia." His voice was full of grit and grime, just like the mega-city it had dwelled in for so long. With that, he played two red cards to claim his first route. Marin tapped the chess clock, and Lilia's timer began to tick ominously.

Lilia let it tick soundly away. She had known Marin a long, *long* time, and he would have been a different man entirely if he let a timer dictate his actions. It was a power play that would have worked well on some of the others she had been imprisoned with, but not with her.

"And what game *are* we playing, exactly?" The timer still ticked away, melting into the sounds of rain and thunder.

Marin chuckled. "The game we always play, Lilia. Risk and reward." He leaned over the table and pressed the timer. Lilia thought he looked disappointed.

It wasn't a good sign.

Marin took another go, drawing a couple of cards, and pressed the timer again to indicate that it was her turn again.

She did not make the same mistake twice, and quickly drew two cards.

They went back and forth in silence for a while. The air was soaked in tension, permeated only by the increasing rage of thunder outside and the creak of the window panes as they held the fury back.

"When were times ever simple, Lilia?"

Lilia looked out at the greyness outside. The rain seemed to be easing off a little. A speck of light peeked nervously through the clouds. She mused on the question for a moment, then gave him a pearly smile.

"You have met my grandchildren, Marin."

"I have."

"You have played games with them. *This* game with them."

Marin's shark-like smile softened. For a moment he almost looked agreeable.

Almost.

"When the summers were long and the laughter was loud," he said with genuine fondness. He took his turn, placing four silver carriages on a second route leading out of the centre of the Gothenburg Mega-Sprawl down to the Copenhagen District, then tapped the top of the timer.

"Hannah is twenty now," Lilia said quietly. She *still* wasn't quite sure what Marin wanted from her, so tried to balance her thoughts between providing meaningful conversation and thinking strategically about her moves. "*Eliksir* officially offered corporate sponsorship to her to study Digital Research." She draw more cards then politely pinged the timer to signal that her turn was over.

Marin snorted- through derision, disgust or anger, Lilia couldn't tell. He steepled his fingers and stared towards the board. Minutes ticked by as Lilia wondered what the focus of his thoughts were.

More minutes ticked by.

Marin ran his fingers through his grey, grey hair and looked down. When he looked back up, the shark-like smile had returned.

Tick tick tick tick tick.

"Where does the time go?"

Marin drew two cards and clicked the timer off. He held up two fingers and beckoned over the guard with the katana. "Get rid of this."

The guard took it without a word. He then handed it off to another of his colleagues. They moved out of Lilia's view. She felt frustrated that she didn't understand what was going on. Marin seemed to sense this, and let out a chuckle.

"Now is the time to focus, Lilia. Focus on what really matters." He pointed at the board. "Your move."

Lilia hesitated.

Focus on what really matters.

Does this really *matter?*

Her hand moved automatically to the draw pile to collect two cards. One was red, one orange, she thought. *Focus on what really matters.* Marin meant the game, clearly. His turns went quicker and quicker. Through muddied thoughts she could see his strategy.

All routes lead to Gothenburg.

Especially the higher scoring ones. Every turn he took, he was aiming to take one of the five routes leading out of the sprawl. If he managed to block her off, victory was all but impossible. He wanted to play against her, to compete. Maybe he was giving her a chance. She could only hope that it was a chance of freedom.

She had to win.

Focus on what really matters.

The words resonated within her once again, echoing like a church bell ringing in the distance. Every time she took a move, or tried to contemplate a strategy, those words steered her thoughts away.

The game grew smaller. Pitiful.

Focus.

Children. Grandchildren. *Hannah.*

Great-grandchi-

"Hannah has a child of her own now, too," Lilia blurted out, breaking the silence with excited whispers. "A little boy. *Beautiful* little crop of blond hair." Lilia's eyes shone with pride.

"He *loves* these sorts of things-" she pointed towards the board. "-too young to play this particular one, though. At the moment." Lilia smiled. "Hannah is playing her part, raising him on the classics. There is a wonderful little tile game, with rivers and castles and fields-"

"I know it well," Marin replied. He continued to listen intently as they traded stories and turns. The storm abated, replaced by a warm glow of oranges and yellows as the sun forced its way through the clouds. Lilia was facing the window; from this high up, she could just make out the crush of industrial buildings that made up the ghettos below.

Time moved on. Now she had started, Lilia could not stop telling Marin about her great-grandson. It burned her heart to think the last time she saw them may very well be the last time.

Lilia screwed her eyes shut and squeezed the idea out and away from her mind. She reopened them, and took a long, hard look at the board.

She was winning.

Her heart stopped burning and started racing. *I must win. For them. I must see them again.*

Marin claimed two more routes to her one in the proceeding few rounds, and Lilia forced herself to fall quiet. The sunlight through the wall of windows made the temperature in the room simmer. Lilia started to sweat.

"Why did you betray me, Lilia?"

"You betrayed me," Marin repeated. His eyes were steel. Lilia met his metal stare with one of her own.

"You changed the rules, Marin."

Marin's fist *slammed* down hard on the table with a horrendous smack. Pieces jumped in front of them and scattered for cover, ruining the current progress of the game. Lilia winced a little, but did not break her eye contact.

"Do not *insult* me, Lilia," Marin said. His voice was raised, and filled with anger and loathing. He pushed away from the table and Lilia braced herself for a hit, or even a shot. Instead, Marin strode away from her, back towards the window, with his arms outstretched.

"*This-*" He gestured out the window. "-is *my* house. The rules are *mine* to change."

The previously unmoved guards scurried over to the table to reset the wayward carriages back on the board. Lilia was impressed with their memory- each piece was placed back exactly where it had been just a moment ago.

She continued to watch the guards as Marin moved back to his seat. His smile was no longer there. Lilia no longer cared.

"You treat it all like these games, Marin. You-"

"-You misunderstand," He said, cutting her off loudly. The calm tones in his voice had quivered in retreat, letting the anger step up to the forefront. "Business is a game. And this-" He pointed down at the board.

"This game is *also* business. *Everything* is business." He snatched a couple of cards from the pile and glared at her. "Of everyone from your little *group*, I would have hoped you could remember that."

None of them returned.

Lilia pondered her next move carefully. If she could rile him further, it might throw him off his game, might give her the best chance to win.

A lot of 'ifs' and a lot of 'mights.' She could not guarantee it though. Marin might just end it right now if she went too far. She had known him and his temper for *far* too long.

"You are angry," she whispered as she gently placed five carriages, one after another, on the route from Gothenburg to Kaliningrad. When she had finished her turn, she placed her hands on top of his. "I apologise."

He did not snatch his hands away like she expected. Instead, he let out a small sigh and lifted his eyes from the table. It was a look of disappointment.

"You betrayed me, Lilia. Apologise for that."

Lilia let the look wash over her for a moment.

Without another word, she took her hands away and placed them on her lap.

For a time, they sat in silence.

"We were fine just transporting goods," Lilia eventually said. She had completed her two destination tickets and leaned across the table to draw another. Marin twitched, and for a moment she thought he was going to grab her hand and stop her.

He didn't. Lilia figured that meant she might still be winning; she had lost track of it in all the commotion. She still didn't know what 'winning' actually meant for her, but the emphasis Marin had placed on victory during the course of the game gave her hope that it might mean her freedom.

"*Just* transporting goods was never the plan. It never brought in the type of money we wanted," Marin snapped.

"You could have used robots!" Lilia exclaimed. Marin spat on the floor at the suggestion. His personal guard swooped in with a cloth to clean up.

"Or cyborgs, Marin! People specifically *designed* for just this type of thing!"

Marin's look soured even further. He placed yet another route on the board, almost twisting the pieces into place. Lilia glanced at his remaining pieces and noted he did not have many pieces remaining. *The game will be over soon.* She started doing some quick maths in her head when Marin interrupted her thoughts.

"I do not deal with *abominations*."

Silence.

Lilia started calculating again. From what she could gather from the state of play, Marin had placed more routes, but Lilia had completed at least one more Destination Ticket than him. She guessed that he was winning, and it scared her. Her mouth went dry and her breath became ever so slightly ragged.

This will soon be over.

"You betrayed me, Lilia."

His hurting tones grated on her. *He has no right to be hurt.* Lilia took a deep breath and pushed her fear from her body. She could not let it stop her from telling Marin what he needed to hear.

"Women, we could deal with. *I* could deal with. I could help them, listen to them, *advise* them."

"Convince them," Marin cut in.

"They could *understand* what it meant to sign a contract with the *great* Marin Vasiliev," Lilia carried on. Her voice quivered but she held her nerve.

"*Children* don't understand."

She quickly placed another three carriages on the board and stared intently at it. Her breathing was shallow again. She focused harder, as if trying to bore a hole in the table. If she thought about anything else, about what she and Marin and the others had done over the years, she knew she would break down.

"I gave them a life, Lilia-"

The tears began to fall. "-You tore them away from their families! Sons away from mothers, daughters ripped from fathers." Lilia growled. *"Grandchildren away from grandparents."*

Lilia crossed her arms on the table and buried her head in it. When she finally spoke, her voice was a harsh, hoarse whisper, as if she had been physically

134

choking back the tears for decades and decades and decades. She kept her head nestled in the crook of her arms, unable to face the monster that sat across from her, the monster she had known, she had aided for the best part of fifty years.

"They thought they were playing a game, Marin."

Marin did not say anything.

Your silence condemns you, Marin.

The quiet angered her. Lilia lifted her head up and pushed her hair back from in front of her eyes, then smeared the tears away with the palms of her hands.

"They thought they were playing a game," she said with a hard sniff. "They thought they were playing. Having fun." Marin's mouth opened at little, as if to interrupt, but Lilia did not dare give him the chance.

"Instead, you used them up and threw them away, and they didn't *understand. They will never understand.*" Lilia pushed out a long, heavy sigh. The weight of years and years of guilt lifted from her shoulders.

"I can never forgive you for that."

Sweat beaded on Marin's nose. The old man sucked at his teeth and blinked. The bead dripped slowly onto the table. One of the guards with a cleaning cloth rushed up to wipe it away. Marin let him. He looked past Lilia as he spoke.

"You do not understand, Lilia. I do not need your forgiveness. I never needed your forgiveness. This is just… it's just *business*."

Lilia leaned back in her seat. No one else in the room would have picked up on it, but there it was, behind the eyes suddenly filled with fatigue, smuggled beneath the ire and the anger.

He was hiding something.

Lilia had known him since they were children, and in all those years together, Marin had never been shy about sharing his thoughts with his peers. The frank openness set him apart from many other *entrepreneurs* within the metropolis, was one of the reasons they had all gone into business together.

"Marin-" she started.

"Get out." The words spiked through the air like needles skewering fabric.

Lilia made to move, but he waved her back in her place. "Not you."

He pointed in the air, made a circular motion with his finger and then gestured at the door. "All of *you*. Outside. Now." The four guards moved without words and without protest. The last one to leave closed it with a heavy *thunk*.

Citrus fermented in Lilia's nostrils once again. It made her feel ill, and Lilia swallowed hard it to make the feeling pass.

I have to get through to him. I have to make him listen.

She had done it before, on more than one occasion. All she had to do was do it all again. *Sommelier.*

The rest of their business partners had toyed with many different roles, trading them with each other as easily as if they were collectable cards.

All of them except Marin and Lilia.

Marin *always* had the final say on things. It was as simple as that. Lilia on the other hand, had always been considered the sommelier of the group.

Her expertise was not wine, though. Lilia had the rare gift of being able to see all sides of a discussion at once. She would sit on the fence and swish them around in her head, picking out the palatable details until she had found the best option for them. She would then present that option to the group, as easily as choosing a wine with dinner.

It was *always* the best option for them, even if it was not the most popular decision at the time. Luckily, Lilia's skills also included persuasion, and backed up by a reasonable and logical argument, not many people could fight against her for long.

For instance, when they were twenty, it had been Lilia who had been given the deciding vote on whether they signed their first major shipping contract with *Génétique*, one of the sprawl's biggest corporations. The contract was lucrative, and would have made them all very, *very* rich very, *very* quickly.

It would have also meant losing their business, with all of them reduced from promising high flyers to permanent members of the pharmaceutical company's workforce. The emphasis had been on *permanent*. It was clear - to Lilia at least - that any resident intellectual property within them would have been thoroughly wrung out of them until they could think no more. Then they would have been thrown into the bowels of the company to live out a life of obscurity.

He had not wanted to listen that day, she thought, as they both sat in disconcerting quiet. *He had wanted to just sign the damned thing and get his hands on the cold, hard cash.*

She had taken Ahna's side in proceedings. With Marin - and others - seething in the background, Lilia had calmly reached forward, taken the contract from his grasp, handed it back to the *Génétique* Board of Directors and bid them farewell.

He had not wanted to listen, but he did. In the end.

They had continued out on their own, using information from each corporation against the other

138

for their benefit. From time to time, Lilia had even encouraged dipping into more niche opportunities, encouraged the subtle blending of black and white until they were no longer two separate colours.

It was all about survival then, as it was now.

"This is just business," Marin repeated softly. His voice was quiet, but it had regained the gritty assuredness that she was accustomed to. Despite the volume, it still had the power to abruptly snap her back into the room from her trip down Memory Lane.

"If this was just *business*," Lilia replied with more than a hint of anger, "You would have folded the company when we all walked away." She thought about pointing a finger at him, then changed her mind. "Instead, you dragged Ahna outside and shot her like a stray. You had Leon *lynched* in the middle of the Malmö Arcology for heaven's sake.

"One by one, you hunted us down, stuffed us into that box of room and-" she gestured with a thumb behind her at the door. "-and you made them do your dirty work.

"If this was just business," she whispered, forcing Marin to lean in close. "You would have joined us out on the streets and taken it like a man."

Marin's jaw was clenched so tightly that Lilia was just waiting for the *crunch*. His left-hand fist was squeezed open and closed just as hard, like a prize boxer warming up. His eyes burned a hole right through her.

Lilia, however was calmer now; with the guards gone, she felt like his equal again, felt like she could suade him once again. She dared to lean forwards slightly, examining her remaining playing pieces a little closer. Lilia twiddled a finger on the back of one of her remaining carriages, quietly whistling to herself.

Marin realised what she was doing and scoffed. Scoff turned to cough- a heavy, throaty cough. Marin pounded his chest and hawked a glob of phlegm onto the carpet next to him. The bright sun dipped behind the clouds as he stomped the mess into the carpet, and all the colours in the room turned to muted stone.

"The rules are mine to change, Lilia. For the longest of times, I did not think they were. You showed me how much *grey* there actually was in this world. Tucked away in forgotten pockets of the city, our little company had so much potential. With the right people, in the right circles, we could have been *kings*."

"I did not intend for my business to entail human *trafficking*, Marin."

Marin gave her a wicked grin that cut from ear to ear. He picked up a carriage from the table and starting twisting it between his fingers. "Not trafficking, Lilia. *Never* trafficking. *Strategic repositioning.*" He placed the carriage, along with three others, down on the board.

"That is what your legacy will be in all of this, Lilia. *Strategic repositioning.* Whatever you *intended* it to be does not matter."

The brief respite from the rain came to an abrupt end. Once again, it tapped insistently on the panes of glass behind Marin.

Think about what really matters.

"And what about you, Marin? What will *your* legacy be?"

There was another long pause between them.

"Whatever you may think, *you* don't get to decide what people remember about you, either. You could be the richest, most powerful man in the world, and you still don't get to choose.

"Now *my* legacy, Marin, is in the hands of my children -my grandchildren - and when it's all been said and done, I am hopeful that their tales of me will be filled only with love and laughter. Do you think Hannah will tell her son about her grandma's kindly old friend Marin after she finds out all you have done?"

The look she gave him was a pitying one. Unless something had changed *very* recently, Marin had no children of his own to speak of.

"Those men out there, how old are they? Twenty-five? Thirty, maybe?"

Marin acknowledged her question with a stoic nod. "So?"

"Do you think they will remember you as a kind man, or as the one who forced them to kill? Which tales do you think they tell? Which ones keep them awake at night? Not the ones you want them to remember, you know."

Marin scrunched up his face, lifted himself from his chair and moved towards the window.

"*Your* legacy belongs to *them*, and it will be one of blood."

Lilia waited for Marin to turn around and berate her. Instead, he continued to look out into the rain. Only his darkened reflection stared back into the room.

"They will fight for your favour until you pick your favourite and leave it all to them. *If* there is any room in your legacy after all the misgivings, misdeeds and murder, it will be filled by the number of zeroes on the end of your share price and only that."

The breath left Marin with a long, sad sigh. He placed a hand on the glass, and they both watched as it slowly fogged around the heat of his fingertips.

Lilia had never seen him so lost.

"*If* what you say is true," Marin finally said. He had not moved except to move his hand from the glass and place them both behind his back. "I shouldn't worry about shares taking up much room at all."

Lilia thought he sounded matter of fact, but when he eventually turned to face her, she noticed how *old* he was. His eyes still held a stubborn fire, but his back was crooked, and he shuffled back to his seat rather than stride over with his usual confidence.

"The business is not where I want it to be, Lilia."

It was a small admittance, but an important one.

"You mean it is failing?"

Marin slowly blinked. It was as close to a 'yes' that anyone was going to get.

"It's all your fault."

"Excuse me?" Lilia said with exasperation. *I thought I had got through*. His sudden change in temperament was not entirely unexpected, based on their meeting so far, but she had hoped for a little bit more candid talk before he lapsed back into the bravado and craved the superiority he knew was slipping away.

 "It's all your fault," Marin snapped once more. He hobbled back to the table and furiously whipped two cards from the deck. Admitting his weakness had made him defensive, and when Marin got defensive, he got angry. "When you left, the rest soon followed."

"No Marin, it was your fault. You knew the issue at hand, yet you pressed blindly on. You were never going to change, and so one by one we left."

Lilia angrily picked up a couple of pieces from the game and placed them on the board. "You drove us away, Marin. You drove *everyone* away. *Then*, you wheeled me out here and played the godfather when really it is *you* who needs *me*. Did you do this with all of them?"

Marin glared at her.

"None of them answered my questions."

"You could have just talked to us! Like partners!" Lilia hissed.

Like friends.

His face had turned cherry red, and his expression was a confused mass of anger, hatred and desperation. The rain had become fierce again, thanks to another storm brewing over the spires of the city.

After decades of being the steadfast rudder of a multinational, Marin Vasiliev was in the water and struggling to keep his head above the surface.

He had been on top of the pile all on his own, and he had pushed everyone else away and continued to enjoy it. With his business faltering and the sharks amassing, the stress of loneliness was at its most potent.

As she watched him pulsate, she knew how much it had changed him- and not for the better. If he had been anyone else, Lilia would have run over to him and squeezed him so hard that he would be left in no doubt that everything was going to be ok. Instead, she looked him in the eye, leaned back in her chair.

"You have become old and vile, Marin."

The light that had been their friendship was swiftly snuffed out.

Marin's lips pressed tightly together in more of a snarl than anything else, and his knuckles turned white from crushing his hands together in silent fury. He reached out to his pieces. *Two left.*

The last turn.

He placed one final route - a little one from the Bothnian Reclamation to Stockholm - and folded his arms across his chest. He looked from the board to Lilia, and snorted loudly.

Lilia blinked a couple of times, then looked down at the completed board as well. This one didn't have a score track around the outside of it like other versions. Instead, it was down to the players to compare and calculate scores afterwards. It was more tense that way.

When Marin didn't move, Lilia quickly started counting up the routes and their relevant scores. Marin was just ahead. They placed their destination tickets on the table- Marin's three to her four- and she added the scores to the pile.

She had won.

Hope spread through her body like heat on a winter's day, and Lilia made to stand up.

"Guards!"

The hope evaporated as Marin's four men rushed into the room. Lilia promptly sat down before anything else could happen. She could see the cogs turning in Marin's head again, turning so furiously that he was likely going to explode.

"No one else will even *think* to mourn you when you are gone."

She had said it in barely a whisper, but she knew that he had heard. The twisted old man balled up his fists over and over and over and his breath grew ragged. Spittle ran from the corner of his mouth as he turned to the guard with the katana.

"She doesn't get a bed. She doesn't get to leave. She gets one meal a day until she changes her tune."

Lilia watched him summon the remainder of his strength and march over to the door. He turned back into the room and pointed to one of the other guards, then over to the board on the table. "That one comes with us. She will have another one."

He looked at her and spat into the room.

"To help her *think*."

With that, Lilia Volkov was left alone. The door closed behind them with a heavy *thunk*. She presumed that Marin's favourite swordsman had remained outside, but when she was sure that Marin had gone, she walked over to the wall of windows and sagged down against them. She closed her eyes and breathed deeply. Seconds, maybe minutes passed.

Lilia opened her eyes and looked into the room. They lingered on the table which had played host to their little game. She had not heard anyone enter, but Lilia was not surprised to see that the beautifully bronzed edition had been replaced by a common copy.

She slowly moved to the table and sat in the chair - *her* chair, she supposed.

It is still a prison cell, she thought, *but it has a view, at least.* Her hands toyed absently with the pieces in front of her. They were cheap and plastic, and flexed beneath her fingertips.

A view, entertainment, and another day to watch the sun rise. Others have come out of a meeting with Marin with less.

The thought made the tears fall once more, and her melancholic laughter filled the space, loud and unbidden.

———

Originally from Birmingham in the UK, and now based in Cardiff, P.E. Pryce has recently finished writing (and is seeking a publisher for) his first novel 'December Rising.' You can follow him on Twitter at ww.twitter.com/ PEPryce.

STARFARM!
by Chris Tannhauser

Setup: Please follow the numbered steps precisely—failure to do so will result in degenerate play and embarrassing Internet posts.

She liked farming; he preferred stabbing things in the neck. They always sat at separate tables, never together because they both played with yellow, the color of the sun, of bananas, a certain flower, happy faces; yellow, the color of liver failure, of pus, a hobo's tooth, cowardice. Beyond this they were barely aware of each other. She knew he was there because he was comfortable around women; he knew she was there because of the unfortunately insistent wetware in his head that was constantly pointing out that her shape was THE MOST IMPORTANT THING IN THE UNIVERSE, a living, breathing Venus of Willendorf constantly snagging the corner of his eye. That, and she said things that made him smile inside.

But on this night they arrived simultaneously late at the *Are You Game?* café, a bright, well-lit place, appointed in blonde wood, spacious, yet pleasingly cluttered like a benevolent wizard's study, smelling of subtle cleaning products, gurgling espresso, and washed bodies. It was trafficked mostly by young, unattached professionals and a small, but hard, knot of grumpy wargamers possessed of gray beards and social mores that might have been shockingly progressive when they were young but were now, buried as they were under a mass of calendar pages, vaguely unsavory. They gathered, that ancient coterie, to silently squint at the most unappealing games imaginable—four-color paper maps with stacks of carefully trimmed cereal-box cardboard squares—meetings punctuated by frequent smoke-breaks where the primary topic of conversation seemed to be upcoming funerals.

And so, through the sin of unpunctuality, it was just the two of them—and the Disaster Twins, the two guys no one ever played with if they could help it. They weren't twins, exactly, but they made no effort to not dress alike, all the while sporting identical barber college haircuts. Perhaps they cut each other's hair. Simultaneously. It was hard to tell. One of them was an unabashed nose-picker who would have done well to channel that fastidiousness into other areas of hygiene; the other held eye contact too long and too hard, the way tigers watched crowds at the zoo—only without the comfort of a glass and steel barrier. From all this it would be easy to assume that they were merely neurodiverse, processing the world differently at a fundamental level, but it was more likely they were choosing—as much as one can call it a choice—to be the living symptoms of a parade of fucked-up Christmases, Santa a no-show, or drunk and gropey when he was there, and the kind of person that might come out of all that. Times two.

She looked at him, and the Twins. "Well," she said, "if we're gonna do this, we might as well farm." She indicated a copy of *Loam Lords: 1401 AD* on the table.

The Twins groaned. He shared their sentiment but kept it to himself.

"1401? Everyone knows 1846—'Luck of the Irish'— is the superior version," said one of the twins with a snotty lilt.

"Yeah," said the other one, "you want fries with that? 'Cause you're not getting fries with that."

"Charming," she replied. "Look, none of us are happy about this. But we make do or no one plays anything."

He raised a hand slightly. "I'm—a little bit happy," he said.

She raised an eyebrow slightly. "Don't get *too* happy," she replied.

They sat and unboxed the thing. Everything was double-sleeved in bespoke plastic like a dubious boner at Howard Hughes' grandma's house. You could spill an entire beer or murder an incontinent hagfish on it and still resell it as mint.

She fumbled a shuffle and cards sluiced across the table. "Jesus, sleeves?" she said, "Someone's afraid their game's gonna get the herpes."

He glanced at the nose-picker. "It might."

Of course everyone knew how to play—who doesn't know how to play *Loam Lords*? It was, after all, *the* game that had cracked the code for heavy strategy gamers and casual non-gamers alike. High rollers and wheelchair-bound luminaries fought million-dollar duels over it in Vegas even as Internet celebrities noodled with the bits while frying on MDMA. It was every baby's first game, and great-grandpa's last; it was the only non-chess game known to have caused a chess master to cane another one into a coma. It had decisions so meaningful they made grown men weep, and yet it was so accessible that even the stupid could wrap their insufficient minds around it. It was quantum mechanics with a pink-sparkly pistol grip.

Setup was perfunctory—eight hands wove the thing precisely, perfectly, out of the chaos of box contents; the first player was obvious, and wordlessly chosen, the first card-fall and chit-push a combination of historically safe opening and shockingly novel gambit. *Gasps and nods all around.* And so they played, the game neatly compressing time and hypnotically transporting them into separate heavens of pure thought, math giving rise to movement and music, to dance and worlds, and a distantly ticking cosmos...

When he chanced to glance up he kept his eyes on her eyes, but not too much; *it's like the sun, like looking at the sun.* You only get a couple seconds. No wonder perceptive women thought all real men were rape-beasts—but hadn't he read something about how it wasn't his fault? That there were ancient monkey circuits whose only job was to wait and wait and wait and then fire like mad when they saw breasts? Circuits that were cultivated, like carnal bonsai, by higher-order Puritan programming, reaching down through the murk of evolutionary history to pull it out by the roots, but instead strangely reinforcing it, making it smaller, but far tougher, bent against the wind? And so heterosexual American males got erections when they saw a baby eat.

Besides, the article was probably written by a lecherous old adjunct professor on his way out the door astride one too many sexual harassment complaints, peer reviewed by other creeps who realized they were going to need something for their lawyers to wave in the faces of an irrational jury. "Blame God," they'd say, "blame the muck we rose from. Blame Science."

"What are you doing?" she asked.

He jumped. "What."

"It's your turn."

He looked at her blankly.

"Sow, reap, prima nocta, something, *anything*."

He blushed, scanned the board, nudged a cube without really thinking—and kicked the game square in the nuts.

"Seriously?" yelled one of the Twins, "*Seriously*? You're gonna ship sorghum *now*?!"

"Sweet Jesus," breathed the other Twin.

"I'll—I'll take it back," he said.

"Oh—oh no, no takesies-backsies. If you're taking it back then I'm taking like my last *ten turns* back, shipping fucking sorghum." The Twin spat the words. "Like you haven't been playing this game your whole fucking life."

"Disrespectful is what it is," said the other Twin.

He didn't look at her again as she used the last of the game to wipe his mess off the board with their stupid faces, tripling all their scores.

1: If you're reading this you've already opened the box, so we'll just skip that part.

How to describe her beyond a simple sigh?

She wore her long, thick hair in sculptural braids that were never the same twice; her deep, bright eyes taking it all in from behind minimalist glasses; her curves draped in loose blouses and skirts that were just this side of Renfaire garb: wide belts, pouches instead of a purse, knee-high leather horse-riding boots. She smelled of vanilla, peaches, and sometimes peppermint. The total effect was intoxicating, amplifying, the difference, he imagined, between merely looking at cocaine and freebasing with a comedian. She was Richard Pryor on fire.

And it made him wish he were that brave. He wore what the other engineering students wore in college, what they still wore at work entirely out of habit: whatever their mom bought them, whatever they found in the drawer, paired-up and color-coordinated, blue with blue, brown with brown, nothing black at all. A frisky day might involve cargo shorts and flip flops with socks, like Cool Craig down in Compliance Testing. He was a dork, too, but somehow he could put it in a box and get laid. There were only two thoughts whenever Cool Craig sashayed into a room: (1) That's totally what I'm wearing for Frisky Friday, and (2) I bet his alarm clock is a blowjob. They would have built a solid-gold statue of him, to the absolute limits of the catastrophic intersection of mass, malleability, compressive strength and structural integrity (which was precisely 3.14158 meters tall, including, of course, his upraised arm calling all dorks forward to bang) if they hadn't hated him in equal measure.

It only took him three weeks to realize that being on time meant they would never play together again—on account of the lack of overlap in their preferred gaming styles, and that whole "yellow" thing—so on the fourth week he began to show up late on purpose. It was a carefully calibrated lateness, 17 minutes past the hour, the precise moment they had first found themselves at the same table. It may have been the purest of chance, or an artifact of her situation—the amount of time it took to neatly fold someone else's work mess so it could be unpacked in the morning, or catching every traffic light between *there* and *here*, or even how long it took her to make and eat a hasty sandwich. And so he bet it all on reproducibility, spending those extra 17 minutes—after he was ready to go—sitting bolt upright on his couch, rubbing his adrenal glands smooth like worry stones.

For another three weeks he arrived precisely late—where he would notice she was otherwise engaged and then peel off as the Disaster Twins mucked their game of *Magic* and vectored for him. Three long weeks of no gaming whatsoever, which was the non-gamer equivalent of not breathing until you get brain damage. He could actually feel himself growing stupid, a sensation that began to gnaw at his resolve.

On the fourth week, she met him in the parking lot.

2: Carefully place the board in the center of the play area; having read that, you are legally prohibited from contacting us for a replacement if you screw it up.

"There's something I want to try," she said as they strode purposefully toward the café, "but the designer's kind of a dick."

"Oh, a game," he said too quickly, then, "What makes you say that?"

"Internet would know, but I don't wanna look. Kids, racism, something like that. Either way, he was found dead in Bangkok of misadventure poisoning."

He squinted. "Someone poisoned him?"

"No, it's—" she hesitated, "—the polite way to say 'autoerotic asphyxiation gone wrong'." Her pronunciation was delightfully precise.

"So you mean auto*thanotic* asphyxiation," he replied.

She broadcast a quick emoji, eyes rolled above a small smile. His heart caught it like it was *eggplant* and *peach* stamped over by *unicorn* and the *red, double-underlined 100*, all of which he slapped away hard, replaced with a brief sum of Holocaust survivor tattoo math to keep himself steady.

Once inside, they cut straight to the pyramid of loaner games, tall enough that it made his palms sweat.

"Here we are," she said, pulling a box out from under the pile. Lesser games clunked into the gap.

"*Star farm*," he read aloud.

She gave him a look. "That is not how it's pronounced."

He looked again. "Sure it is. *Star farm*."

"Read it," she said.

"*Star farm*."

"Read it!" she demanded.

"*Star farm!*" he exclaimed quietly.

She threw her hands up over her head and shouted "STARFAAARM!" at the entire room.

"We're game," said one of the Disaster Twins.

The four of them sat together out of common courtesy, and the distant twang of empathy, and a little bit of social anxiety, and a feeling—held weirdly out of phase by all of them—that they were making friends. The box lid came off with a loud fart, and the Twins snickered, and he hated himself for his reflexive approval.

Beneath an archaeology of baggies, the board was one of those scary six-folders where no matter how you tried to unfurl it there was always at least one panel hanging by nothing more than paper and glue and angst. What started with two hands quickly involved all eight, and to no good effect, the Disaster Twins struggling to invoke mad shearing forces even as he and she worked to minimize them; no one present had an ownership stake in the game, making half of them super-careless and the other half super-careful. The overall effect was like watching a crow with a broken wing trying to get into a brightly colored snack bag. Miraculously, they got the thing flat without a tear and only the merest hint of profanity.

Laid out, it was quite a thing to behold, beautifully rendered, a massive art piece first painted on canvas by a delayed suicide, then delicately overlaid with game-boundaries, selection boxes and subconsciously evocative icons. It was the sort of spread that made a True Gamer's breath catch in the throat.

Half of the board was lavish with an asteroid bubble farm, a dome of life on a lonely rock, bright with bucolic colors, sectors for fields and crops, cube corrals and control panels for monitoring atmosphere, water tankage, soil pH, and orders for programming the limited number of robot brains to plow, sow, reap and load outbound shuttles; the other half was dead space, a forbidding void where a science fiction protagonist's parents might go missing, a minimalist star-sprinkled black, sectors for outbound shuttle lanes and occult enemy vessels, dice docks and control panels for monitoring station integrity, railgun tracking, nuclear munitions, and orders for programming the limited number of robot brains—shared with the farming side—to scan, intercept, direct weapons fire and recover inbound shuttles. And the whole shebang, for some reason, bounded entirely by a whimsically-scrolled roll-and-move track around the perimeter.

As the eye lingered, further details emerged, creating the illusion of descending toward the station, nose pressed to the fogged glass of a rad-hard porthole. The landscape was alive with tiny activity, people and thinking machines working hand-in-glove to produce the raw foodstuffs necessary to make million-credit hamburgers for distant pockets of human life where scarcity and circumstance allowed for the neat intersection of need and greed—you think you wouldn't do much for an apple, but you'd be surprised at the indignities you'd suffer if your only other option was yet another bowl of your fellow colonists' hydrolyzed feces. And there, in a nascent star-lit orchard, stands a robot offering that red, shiny apple to a human in an orange jumpsuit and straw hat, the look in their eyes the whole of human history come to this moment. *This is a goddamn space apple, and you will pay handsomely for it.*

"Damn," someone breathed.

"I know," one of the Twins said, "roll and move? Really?"

"And paper money," said the other one, throwing a fat wad of varicolored cash on the table, a kaleidoscope of tiny portraits of the first—*and last*—robot president staring enigmatically back at them, "Cool."

Someone flipped open the rulebook.

"Does... anyone know how to play?" he asked.

The Twins gave him the *I thought you did* look, and she shrugged.

"We'll figure it out as we go," she said.

He died a little inside.

"This'll be interesting," said one of the Twins.

"Always is," said the other.

As they started sorting through the baggies, he noticed the game wasn't sleeved.

"Whoa, whoa, *whoa*—everybody," he said, "the game isn't sleeved, so be super, super careful. What are you—"

She paused, halves of a deck bent backwards in anticipation of the weaving waterfall. "Shuffling," she said.

No no no no no, something inside him screamed.

He took a deep breath. "You have to *pile* shuffle."

She slowly tilted her head to one side. "*Pile* shuffling isn't shuffling. It's pile *sorting*. Use your math, nerd."

He gurgled. "Look I know you're right—but the cards!"

"The cards will be fine," she said, riffling a scrotum-clenching waterfall and return bridge. "They're *made* to be shuffled."

And so they learned the game in the worst way possible, one person reading inexpertly from the rulebook while everyone else interrupted with their own interpretations and assumptions brought in from other games and a vast experience with games in general, everyone convinced of the superiority of their own mastery, most of it right—after a fashion—but the wrong parts were really wrong, so much so it can be said they didn't really play at all.

The game began with one of the Disaster Twins lighting off a nuke, to which other one replied by lighting off two, "Just to see what would happen."

"Well, what you've done," she said slowly, "is waste three nukes while irradiating this entire swath of crops." She hovered a splayed hand over much of the arable land beneath the dome.

"Sorry," said one of the Twins without meaning while the other stamped a hard-edged resource marker across the board like a child's thimble rounding Go.

The rest of the business went as you might expect: two alpha gamers and two desperate damage control drones at each other like people with hands around necks in a house fire, pulses dwindling beneath fingers better served by calling emergency services, but no one willing to be the chump who let go first... So they burned in the plasma flash that breached the hull completely, the explosion reversing as the farm rudely evacuated itself into space. Four more alien destroyers decloaked in the debris cloud, within 500 meters, strafing the fleeing shuttles with impatient smart munitions, signal lost one by one as a chorus of screams became a band, and then a trio, a cruel duet, a solo—heartfelt and affecting—and finally the solar radiation hiss of an unheard John Cage piece.

It was unclear exactly what the aliens did with the survivors holed up in the emergency shelters, as the game handled that hideous denouement behind a mercifully blunt YOU HAVE LOST curtain.

After a bit of nonsensical math the final tally showed a score of $\sqrt{-1}$.

He and she cleaned up the game in silence as the Disaster Twins bickered over the details of the After Action Report, finding fault almost entirely in the fact that while she had farmed alone she had done so ineptly; and that the two of them could have handled the defense of the station if only he hadn't interfered.

He tuned them out, replacing their hectoring with the artistry of her hands, small birds in flight, moving with practiced ease across the gamescape, perfectly proportioned, smooth, scarless, the color of good health, her nails done in a sparkly gunmetal, not chewed to nubs like his were.

"Somebody's gotta get home and bludgeon the ghoul," one of the Twins blurted.

He fumbled the moment, watched it fall away, sickeningly, to shatter against reality. "Excuse me?"

"You know," said the other one, "wander the labyrinth of the Internet until the ghoul peeps out, get your hands around his neck and beat him until his ichor spatters the flagstones. Then see if you level up. Basic *D&D*, my friend."

He flushed, tried to say something in the negative, found the pipeline between his disordered head and his tongue to be hopelessly jammed with competing verbal activity. He looked at her and felt like he always did. She frowned.

"He won't level up," said the other Twin.

3: Shuffle them decks till it hurts—till their edges are worn smooth, their backs curled, their faces greasy with hand-jam; if you use sleeves, don't.

He stopped going to game night. Being near her was an exquisitely specific pain, proof he was incomplete, like finding out you were supposed to have three arms but you only had two and a freshly-shorn, unresolved stump, nerves still vibrating with the shock of disconnection. Part of him wanted to go back to the stump-blind past where he could just sleep and eat and work without knowing, without feeling— whatever this awful thing was.

Another midnight bike ride, more of these lately, pounding into the dark, gliding from pool of light to pool of light, the physical meditation of the body like a Sadhu's mortification, unmooring the mind and allowing it to float free

—the car ran the red light at speed; he was dumped back into his body like a shock of ice water, the brakes squealing low on everything: his skinny tires, the GTO's fat ones, time itself; the reflections of the bright red orbs of the traffic lights floated across the car's glossy candy coat, languorous as bloody soap bubbles, drifting up the windshield to a frozen emoji—sleepy look of nascent surprise—half-lit in the blue of a raised phone showing some random social media feed, thumb poised over a LIKE button, the confluence of time snapping suddenly 1:1 as his front tire kissed the rear bumper of the car, snatching the bike out from under him and flicking him to black—

he woke at the end of the ragdoll sequence, one final roll onto his back beneath a sky punctured by the hard points of actual stars. Fuck it, he thought inside his ruined helmet, I'm going to tell her.

4: Select the start player using any suitable method; but probably not the first one you thought of, because that's kinda stupid.

Being bereft of sophisticated moves, he reached all the way back to elementary school for his next one, a folded note he passed to her without fanfare. She took it easily enough, a part of him reporting that her hand lingered a microsecond too long for such a transaction. Her face gave nothing away.

They played at their usual tables, separated by space and approach, and though he tried he never caught her looking at the note. Or at him.

She returned it at the very end of the night, last minute in the parking lot, coming up behind him as he was stacking boxes in the backseat of his car.

"Hey," he said in surprise.

"Hey," she said, and handed him the note.

He palmed it like an illicit tip and went back to sorting, his face hot. He could feel her receding into the night.

Back at home—sleepless hours later—he finally bolted from bed, snapped on the lights and looked at the folded paper on the dresser. It was curled slightly with the essence of her, from the pleasant moisture of her hands, from resting against small belongings in one of her impossible pockets. He could almost smell the vanilla, or peaches.

Slowly, he reached for it and opened it in the same smooth motion. It read, in Courier 12-point:

```
I like you.  Do you like me?

| | YES

| | NO

| | OTHER:  _____
```

There was a curlicue "x" in the OTHER box, and the words HELL YES on the following line in a unique and practiced hand.

He just about fainted.

5: Roll the dice to determine zxk17unm.

A week later and seventeen minutes after the hour, they were in the parking lot again.

"Let's play," she said with an openness that struck him dumb.

They went straight for *STARFARM!*, and the Disaster Twins met them there.

"Let's play!" one of them said.

He and she barked a simultaneous "No!" that shocked everyone.

"Maybe next time," he said in response to the hard, but familiar, hurt on their faces.

And so he and she sat across from each other at the end of a long table thrumming with activity and began the eternal dance of play.

The world receded by degrees, the problems that are other people, numbers on spreadsheets, doubt and meaning, being a bewildered child in a rapidly putrefying vessel—these things grew small until it was as if they had never existed, replaced instead by a universe where the whole of the rules was smaller than a human mind, a sensation of godhood. In this microcosmic playground they extended, tentatively, the machinery of cooperation; naked, whirling gears seeking their complimentary counterparts in order to mesh without grinding. And in that moment where the expectation was for terrible noise, a fountain of sparks, smoke, the smell of burning metal—there was instead a soundless smoothing out, the glide of machinery connecting with its purpose-built supercharger, action at both ends seamlessly amplified.

It only occurred to him to be terrified later.

But in the all-consuming *now* they played together, every alteration of the gamestate distorting the whole, causing disparate parts to fall inexorably into place, succumbing to the gravity of the thing. You grip, you twist, and everything slides. When he moved he could feel her reciprocating, and weirdly found himself anticipating just what she needed almost simultaneously with her subtle call. If this wasn't telepathy, then there was no magic in the world.

How many hours became a murmur of minutes? It was over too soon, having only just begun—when the chatter of recounted victories, defeats, calls for cheap beer and cheaper food, *just-one-more-game-somewhere-else* rose around them like an obliterating tide. The owner flashed the lights.

They looked at each other with identical expressions, then looked at the board. The mass of cards and cubes and chits and minis and dice were all smeared into the last four-panel page of a graphic novel about people trying to do people stuff where people aren't supposed to be: growing food inches away from black vacuum and hard radiation—a logistical nightmare anyway—further complicated by an inscrutable alien presence acting on principle, or hatred, or raw instinct.

Perhaps, he thought, they fought for what was curled at the core of this nondescript asteroid—a star-scouring artifact hidden away by a failed civilization;

or a slumbering god; or their Voice, stolen by that god, leaving them incapable of anything but annihilation, only understanding the exclamation points of nuclear weapons. Maybe humanity plunked this farm down in a simple graveyard, and the fact that we were absorbing their sacred dead and shipping them off to be consumed by other starfaring apes was an ultimate taboo whose only possible response was genocide. Or they were future humans come back through a web of wormholes to stop the birth of Space Hitler—

"You know why we lost," she said.

He scanned the board. "I got overwhelmed. Expended too many nukes too early. Sorry."

"Hmmn," she said, doing that eyebrow thing.

He woke suddenly in the small hours, pulse quick with realization. *They lost because they both kept overextending for each other.* Instead of masterminding the end of the game, or take-take-taking and leaving the other person to fend for themselves, they kept shoveling resources—turns, cards, robot brains—to the other side of the equation, thoughtlessly, leaving it in a perpetually shifting state of unbalance. He settled back into sleep's embrace, intrigued, strangely comforted, because he could see it there, the outline of a vast continent in fog.

He wondered if she could see it, too.

6: You invited her over? Tell your roommate not to stare. On second thought, give him a movie ticket and an inverse curfew. Also, buying condoms isn't creepy, it's caring.

"Holy shit, your place is clean," she said, marveling at the dentist-office presentation of wiped surfaces, perfect proportions, and horizontal spaces clear of stuff.

"And yours... isn't?" he asked.

"Well, it's not like the bathtub's full of poop or anything; more like, 'lived in' by three cats and a couple monkeys."

"I—see," he said, slightly disappointed, then disappointed at his disappointment.

He produced a serviceable dinner of spaghetti and meatballs from scratch as they spoke deeply, intensely, about games, gaming, and online gamer culture. Over the last of the wine he steered conversation toward the topics recommended by his mom: *God, UFOs, babies.*

"Goddamn babies," she muttered, shaking her head.

"What? I thought women... loved babies."

"Because we have boobs? C'mon."

"The way they smell," he said matter-of-factly.

"Like dirty diaper?"

"The way they cut through the armor and go straight to the thing inside us that goes stupid with cute."

She ignored his unironic earnestness. "Even the ugly ones?"

"There are no ugly ones," he said.

"Internet says otherwise. Google that shit. 'Dot dot dot only a mother could love.'"

"And you don't... want to be a mother?"

She regarded him coolly. "No—"

His face fell; she caught it.

"—but maybe I just haven't met the right sperm donor yet."

The evening proceeded as one might expect. They shook hands when she left.

7: You invited him over? Tell your roommate so she can do the thing. Also, condoms, because this guy is clueless.

"Where's your roommate?" he asked.

"She knows not to be around. We have a system."

"Oh," he said with a minor twinge, "You must do this a lot." He instantly regretted saying it.

"I'm going to ignore that."

Her place *was* "lived in," but not psychotically so; more "Victorian garage sale" than an episode of *Hoarders*.

She whistled and the cats arrived in sinuous single file and sat in a mild semicircle, regarding him expectantly.

She pointed at them one by one. "Tardis, Artoo, Meeple."

"Aw, how cute—Meeple!"

"Of course his name's not Meeple," she rolled her eyes. "Jesus Christ."

He looked at the cats and they looked at him.

 "Mr. Darcy, Bechdel, and that one has no name."

"No Name the Cat?" he asked.

"No, he doesn't have a name. Please don't refer to him otherwise. It's rude."

"Poor guy doesn't have a name?"

She sighed. "He doesn't give a shit. He gets pets and treats and the mouse-chow keeps coming; nothing's going to eat him. He'll probably die of some weird geriatric cat disease his ancestors couldn't dream of. A name isn't even on his list."

"What do you do at the vet?"

She snorted. "They gave him a number."

"What's his number?"

"Nope, not falling for it." She waggled a finger at him. "You will not call him by a number."

Secretly, he dubbed the nameless cat c, not for "cat" but as shorthand for 299,792,458 meters per second, the speed of light in a vacuum.

The evening proceeded as one might expect. They shook—

That's not what happened at all. Exactly *how* it happened he wasn't even sure of; all the usual stuff was going on, easy conversation that shifted between light and heavy topics the way a ridiculously expensive sports car might traverse ess curves up and down a mountain, dinner, some wine, then sitting on a magnetized couch that acted on them like helpless nuts and bolts, sliding inexorably closer until they clacked and there was no getting them apart, a change in the tenor of the evening that took him entirely by surprise even as a part of him realized she knew exactly what she was doing.

She left the lights on, transformed by nakedness, her frame rising proud, as if daring him not to be aroused.

He failed.

She rolled him over, straddled and sat on him. His entire being was wonderfully, horribly, wadded up and yanked out of himself, like a banquet fastidiously laid with white-gloved hands suddenly leaping out a ruptured airlock—you thought you were sitting down to a sumptuous twelve-course meal but instead you got the shock of empty lungs.

She stopped moving and cocked her head at him. "Are you a virgin?"

He hesitated, hated himself for it. "No," he said. "Not anymore."

"Oh, *honey*," she said and kissed him harder and deeper than he thought possible.

I can't breathe, he thought, *and I like it*.

"Now it's my turn," she said, and like most gamers he was very good at following directions.

8: GET READY FOR FOREVER

He got them their own copy of *STARFARM!*, carefully punched, sorted, bagged, laminated and double-sleeved—the thing was absolutely bulletproof, good for a lifetime of plays. In print, out of print, it wouldn't matter. They had their own copy—never to be played by anyone else—a forever game, never the same twice, a nexus of life stages and memory. At least that was the idea.

She farmed; he stabbed things in the neck. Once, they almost switched roles; once, and almost. But the rest of the time they sat down in habit-worn seats, took possession of their respective unworn bits, and meshed their minds like it was nothing in a way that should make you jealous, right here, right now, searching to see if you have ever known this thing in your life. She managed the farm at the edge of optimal, adjusting deftly to shortages, the timing of lifecycles and shuttle schedules, the occasional burst of radiation and breached hulls. She implored him to spare a returning shuttle, incongruently heavy with unknown cargo, "on a hunch"—it turned out to be stowaway refugees. He managed the never-ending war beyond the interface, feints and ruses, ships decloaking, shuttles returning full of ravenous boarders. He husbanded dwindling nukes, finally convinced her to give up an ocean's worth of water for a single ice ship—*the Assumption of Humanity*, starship-class but rigged with rapid-vectoring spaceship motors, a spinal mass driver that could accelerate payloads to a good chunk of c, and the ability to take a pounding the way an ocean swallows storms. She used the calm he afforded to quadruple their foodstuff tonnage.

In celebration, he ordered the five robot brains in charge of the crater-pocked *Assumption* to execute a pants-shitting flyby of the dome—he switched the screen up for an old-school telescope, wanting the photons burying themselves in the back of his eyes to be real reflected light. He saw her then, in her orange jumpsuit and straw hat, handing the apple to a robot, saying, "Look at what you have done, this entirely unlikely thing, to bring a taste of Earth to a far-flung Earth-child."

This was the dance of years.

9: Check for game end condition.

It only took six weeks for the cancer to take her.

The whole time, the whole time, filled with the horrible mixture of what they did for each other and the fear of losing it. Of hope against hope, thinking *this time will be different because it's us*, all the way up to her final shuddered breaths, a look of blind terror on her face even as he held her hand and wished fiercely, with everything he was, it wasn't so.

10: I got nothin'.

Something he had never considered: the perfect dance around funerals, guaranteed with every birth— we howled on the savannah, we howled in caves, we howl in buildings and we will howl tomorrow on distant worlds. This was a groove worn deep by your ancestors; even if you don't know the tune, the groove knows your feet. The first step suggests the next, and so on to the end.

Their families, joined—however tenuously—by what he and she did for each other, brought together now in grief for a long, dull, tearing grind of the grief in others reaching blindly for the grief in him. He endured this black reinforcement until it seemed to suddenly attenuate on its own, and he was alone in their home with the scent of her.

He loosened his tie, stripped it out in a recently practiced motion, discarded it to the floor. He shed his suit coat as he walked to their game room, to the shelves of just the ones they loved, boxes rimmed white with shelf-wear. He ran a finger down their absolute favorites, aware of the slight buzz of texture under the pad, and stopped at *STARFARM!*, removed it from the shelf and set it gently on the table. The top came off like butter and he began to set it up according to the directions, precisely and without the need for reference—on autopilot, really—until the whole thing was good to go, every last sheet, card, pasteboard bit laminated and double-sleeved. Absolutely bulletproof, good for a lifetime of plays.

It was like she had never been there at all.

———

Chris Tannhauser is a hand-to-hand combat instructor from Southern California, who has written three books and hundreds of articles and essays on the topic of practical violence. And though his critics might say otherwise, this is his first piece of published fiction. More of his award-winning, game-related writing can be found on BoardGameGeek (as HiveGod) and for more of his short stories please visit doomthinkequations.blogspot.com.

You Are What You Do

by Anthony Snider

The first shot hits me in the eye. I spiral backwards and fall to the pavement, in shock. Why am I alive? Oh. Right. Because I am made of cardboard. I reach up and gingerly feel my eye, finding the bullet imbedded in my layers. Thin strings of spiralled paper fuzz from the edges of my eye-hole.

I've got to admire the shot. The shooter is across the alcove, on the other side of the street - a good distance - and he snap-shot me right in the eye! I barely saw him. Then again, I am almost literally a paper target now, which I'm sure he's specifically trained to shoot, being a policeman. As I lie wool-gathering (or more literally "cardboard-gathering"), I can hear he has already resumed picking off other targets. He's doing well I guess, because I hear screams, and thuds, and whomps, and other strange sounds. I wonder briefly what this policeman is made of... gunmetal?

I don't think it had to be this way - that he'd necessarily be shooting. Maybe the uniform is incidental. Really, for all I know, he could just be made of hate.

I realize I'm trying to figure out his rules, when I should be concentrating. I have my objective: I need to get home. My children are home by now - sent home early when the crisis occurred. The crisis that's changing us all.

Maybe I can outrun the policeman. I think I've got the action points to do it. Still lying on the sidewalk,

I turn my head, and I can see him. He's lining up to shoot here, then there. He's aiming at random, but now he's not shooting. Maybe he's out of targets. Maybe he's just conserving ammo. How many shots has it been?

When he's looking elsewhere I crawl over and hide behind a double-parked car. Unfortunately, my car is far away, in the parking garage.

I realize he'll notice my body is missing from the sidewalk. Damn. He might come closer to investigate. I'm trying to strategize when I hear a jingling from around the corner of the building.

An obviously homeless man turns the corner. The first shot hits him in the chest, and there's a ricochet. The second shot enters his head - and there's a spray of spare change out of the other side. He crumples. He's sprawled on the sidewalk, in a puddle of coinage and rumpled clothes, but as the coins settle I hear them lightly cursing.

And now someone emerges from my office building - it's my co-worker Beverly.

"Get down Bev!"

She looks down at me just as a bullet hits the glass doors behind her, shattering.

Beverly yelps. She's been slowly turning into a large mastiff for an hour or more - pictures of her dogs have always wallpapered her cubicle, and now she's starting to resemble them. She's crouched now, and the resemblance is nearly complete.

"Come here, Beverly! Over here!" I wave at her, unconsciously using the same voice I might use with a pet.

Beverly looks at me, a mixture of trepidation and sadness on her almost-human almost-canine muzzle. Her brows begin to furrow.

Her fore-paws, still long-fingered, begin to curl into fists. "That son-of-a.." devolves into a grumbling growl.

She charges, loping, in the direction of the shooter!

Shocked, I turn and peek back over the car. The policeman hasn't reacted to her yet. Has he not seen her? Her loping form is obvious. I stand and yell and wave my arms, hoping to distract the policeman - obviously this is a cooperative game now. He aims at me and pauses. He's surprised to see me alive.

I scream louder at him. Amazingly, the homeless man joins in with a jingling chorus. The policeman turns towards him now, confused, and Beverly is upon him.

Her snarls and bites are unwholesome to listen to. The shooter screams in shock as she pounces but he doesn't fire again - maybe he was out of ammo after all. Beverly is all over him now, and the policeman seems to have curled into a defensive ball.

***

The existential crisis began a few hours ago. We could feel things changing. Like the smell of ozone before a storm, we knew something ominous was approaching.

A few minutes later it was as if something bloomed within me. I could feel my interests bubbling up inside, fighting for dominance. I questioned everything. What was important? Art history was pushed aside by graphic design. Graphic design fought a battle with my constant hobbies. My relationships with my two kids and my ex-wife stood aside idly and my purest hobby emerged as the winner. In the end, my skin began to take on a linen texture, with a slight gloss finish. My details smoothed and were replaced by simple info-graphics. The graphic that replaced my stomach was an apple with an arrow pointing to a lightning bolt contained in a circle. Simple, once you know what it means: put food ('apple') here ('arrow') and get energy ('lightning bolt'). Easy. Other action tattoos bloomed over my paper arms and body. They itch slightly.

But I'm "rules-gathering" again. The shooter and Bev are gone. Perhaps Beverly has dragged him off. Or buried him.

I pick myself up. I seem none the worse for wear, with just a bit of fraying at the edges. Practically new in box, except for the eye. My trade value is still pretty high.

It's a quarter mile walk to the parking garage. But a quarter mile is a long way, now that the world is different.

I'm finally on my way; using some movement-points, when I see it. A boulder made of metal. There are cars at the stop-light (maybe it's just not their turn) and a mass of metal - a sphere of sparks and spiking silver shards - is rolling down the street. It bounces onto cars and absorbs them with shrieks of twisting metal and of their drivers. It rolls towards me all edges and spikes and I look frantically for some cover to dive behind, but it turns chasing after yet another car.

I wonder. Is the boulder a car thief? Or maybe a carjacker? What would I do if it returned, once I'm in my car? But I realize I'm trying to figure out strategy again. Stop with the analysis paralysis: Move already!

There aren't any cars left on the street now and I run across into the parking garage.

I've reached my car. I fumble with the keys, my cardboard fingers bending every which way. Finally I get in, and I can't help but look in the mirror. My eye's not so bad really. Just a dull metal center a little too deep in the ink. Some exposed edge layers. The ancient Chinese made armor of layered paper. It gives me character, I think - a new and interesting component.

It's going to be a long drive home. I know my kids' school let out early - I got an auto-text notice on my phone earlier. By the time I get home, my kids should be there. I pull out my phone, but it makes no sense to call now.

There's no traffic on the highway.

I start to calm down, and I know I need to concentrate but I can't help thinking about it. About Everything. I'd like to call home but I doubt my kids are home yet. My kids. I wonder. Alex is my eldest, and personable, and always on his iPhone or social media, or on YouTube. But my youngest is taciturn and mostly in his own world, usually with a book from the Kindle or my bookshelf. If I call now, Alex might answer, but... But what? Never mind. I'll find out, later. I'm driving now.

The empty highway. It's eerie. I punch the radio button. Music. I barely notice the tune.

The highway slow-curves and I'm catching up to an 18 wheeler up ahead - just the cab. It's moving at a good clip, but not really negotiating the curve. I hit the gas, threatening to bend my cardboard leg too much. I'm afraid the huge truck might hit the guard rail.

The radio is interrupted with breaking news.

I'm even with the truck now. There's something sticking out of the driver's side window - a plank of wood maybe.

A news commentator begins babbling.

As I pass the truck, I realize there's a hand nailed into the plank of wood. I turn to bite into the curve.

Apparently there's rioting and madness all over the country. Duh.

I look in the rear view mirror, and I catch a glimpse of the driver - all that wood crammed into the truck's cab - just as the truck hits the guard rail. The tail end of the cab arcs up and over into a perfect flip. The driver's thorny crown slips as the truck flips, smashing through and over the guard rail. The metal screams. The truck flips out of sight, off the elevated highway and down to the roads and buildings below.

The radio mentions that martial law has been declared.

There's a news helicopter hovering well over the highway. I scrunch down in my seat to look up, my cardboard wrinkling uncomfortably.

The pilot, covered in feathers, jumps from the chopper. He flaps frantically. The whirlybird dips, descending with a spin. I gun the gas pedal, creasing my foot badly, but the car won't go any faster.

The pilot, still flapping frantically, arcs up into the wind and out of the way, just as the helicopter drops - right in my path.

I'm not going to beat it. I veer the car into the guard rail. Sparks fan up over the hood, and miraculously, the guard rail opens into an exit ramp. I'm going too quickly, and I slam on the brakes. The car skids and fishtails. There's a smell of burning rubber and the car veers down the ramp just as the helicopter explodes. I'm just below the level of the highway as shards of glass and metal fly overhead. I pump the brakes as burning fuel rains down on the road. Finally the car stops. I'm breathing heavily, so at least I still do that. There's bits of flaming wreckage everywhere.

The radio reminds everyone to stay in their homes or at work. Thanks, radio.

I get out of the car to catch my breath. I wonder how much longer I will still breathe. My legs are wobbly.

I look up at the elevated roadway, held up by massive columns, and I see licks of flame over the guardrails. I'll have to drive side roads until I get back up on the highway past the wreckage. Now would be a good time to call home, but instead I punch the home button on the car's touch-screen gps. It does nothing. Cardboard doesn't conduct electricity. Which means my smart-phone won't work either. Damn.

The air is full of smoke and the smell of burning metal, and I hope the car's undercarriage is not on fire. I really hope. I'm very flammable now I guess. At least I'm not sweaty, since I seem to have lost that ability. I spend an action to get back in the car.

I don't know this area downtown, I usually drive over it on the highway. It's a blight of abandoned warehouses, covered in gang graffiti. It doesn't help that there are patches of burning helicopter littering the area.

I inch the car forward and it's attacked by roaches. Man-sized roaches wearing tattered clothing. There's two or three of them, their chitinous arms reaching for the car handles, having skittered out from nowhere, their long head-feelers whipping at the windshield.

By reflex, I step on the gas, and one of the mansects scampers up onto the hood. He stares at me with bulbous spheres and frantic feelers as the scenery whizzes by, and he tries to pull a gun from out of his belt, but I turn a hard left. He buzzes and is gone, his many legs flailing.

I turn onto a couple more side roads, but I'm going too fast for these short turns and I pump the brakes. No bugs in the rear view. I resume my regular turn.

I drive lost for a while under the highway's shadow, from side-road to backroad. Where am I? Where do I belong? I start to think of my kids and I spot an on-ramp.

As I get back on the highway a building behind my car crumbles. The entire building. Into dust. I know I drove by it, but I don't remember the building. I wonder if it was important. I drive up the ramp.

The highway here is littered with wrecks. A car on its side. A pickup truck up on the guardrail. A motorcycle perched weirdly on the tripod of its handlebars.

I drive with trepidation until I see a man splayed out on the road. He's wearing a motorcycle helmet. He starts to sit up.

I know I should keep driving, but it could be a temporary emerging alliance, and he is partially blocking the road. I roll down the window.

"You all right? You hurt?"

He gives me a salute. He hops up, perfectly nimble, and runs over to the car, "I could use a ride!"

"Where... are you headed?" I ask him, but he's already getting into the passenger side. "That way!" He points in the direction the car is already pointed. I notice his dusty clothes might have the vague hint of stars underneath inches of road grime.

I spend more movement points and the highway is clear up ahead and we're off at a good clip.

"So what happened back there?" I ask him.

"It didn't go so well, but I'm sure this time will be better."

"What didn't...?"

And he grabs the wheel. The car does the impossible - instead of lurching to the side, it launches up and forward at an incredible speed, over an unseen impossible ramp. We're slammed down into our seats and the car is lifted into the air.

I turn to him but his helmet is unreadable. There's the sick sense of cresting over a hill, and now the car is falling. We're both lifted up out of our seats and he yells, "brace yourself!" and the car smashes back down on the highway. My boneless limbs flap, and the airbag explodes just as the radio crackles ,"a new record!"

By the time the airbag deflates, the motorcyclist is gone. We appear to have jumped an incredible distance, and the radio non-sequiturs, "...easily broken the previous record!" before returning to the news of our current apocalypse.

But I'm much closer to home.

The car makes a deep grinding sound. I get out of the car and an actual tie-fighter flys by with a distinctive whine, and I wonder how a hobby or obsession results in a huge unlikely physical object like that. I make a wish but nothing seems to happen. I scratch my head with my cardboard fingernails. Oh well.

The car is kaput. I realize how close I am to home. Instead of following the arc of the highway, I can walk across a short field, go through the public park, and cross a few residential streets to get to the house.

The park is unusually crowded. I see a jogger barefoot running, their feet and legs having grown disproportionately huge to their shrunken torso. There's a group of teens playing basketball, morphing together into an amorphous blob. I pass a man whose head has sprouted four propellers. He's fiddling with his own remote.

I leave the park and cross the gated footbridge at the end of my street. It's only a short walk to my house. I'm anxious to go inside but I hear someone yell my name.

Jay, the local lawn guy, the gossip, runs over to me from across the street where his riding lawn mower is parked. I'm taken aback. I look at him, but I can't see any obvious changes at all.

"Well, look at you now!" Jay declares. "What are ya, a newspaper or somethin?"

"Uh, look Jay. I'm really tired and I'd like to get home, okay?" I start to reach for the door.

"Whoa there! I'm just bein' neighborly is all. Look, I just think you should take a quick breath before you go inside."

I stare at Jay, his bald, but untanned, and surprisingly white head hidden under a ball cap. "What are you getting at Jay?"

"Well now. I'm just sayin' that when a man has has an experience like today has been, maybe he should slow things down a bit is all."

Jay is being cagey, and I don't like it. Like when he's buttering me up to increase his lawn-care prices. What's he on about?

"I've been outside most of this late August day, I have. And I've seen a few things today a might uncommon you could say."

No kidding Jay. Today's all kinds of uncommon.

"What have you seen, Jay? I need to get inside with my kids."

"Well there's that. That is to say... look. Look over there."

Jay gestures one house over and towards the parked car. I'd taken no notice of it. It's my neighbors car, and like most days he's under it fiddling around. His feet are sticking out. There's something off about his shoes, but I don't really have time for... they have gears. The treads of his shoes are gears, and they are turning.

"Don't go in your house," says Jay earnestly. "I saw your kids get off the bus earlier."

My breath is caught in my throat.

"And I bet you were hoping..."

There's something wrong with Jays mouth.

"...that your kids were too young to be affected by this thing..."

I was hoping that. And Jays mouth is strangely full.

"...but I seen 'em, and I'm here to tell you, that kids were affected more than adults, not less."

There is a giant eyeball in Jay's mouth. As he talks you can see the huge iris just behind his tongue. Most of his head must be filled with that eye. And it's directly attached to his mouth.

I again reach for the door.

"Alright. But don't say I didn't warn you."

Jay turns as he leaves. As he turns, I can see the edge of his face. His hat sits on top, and the mask of his face is on the front, but his whole head is that one single eye. And he says the kids are worse.

I open the door.

Alex is there. I feel sick. Alex has no form. He's a mass of floating images and internet memes swirling around themselves interspaced with ad traffic and pop up menus. He's a riot of pixels and video and thumbs-ups, and he's hovering over his iPhone.

"Hello, son. I'm home."

"Much Hello, father! So much greetings!" says a tempest of doge headshots swirling over the couch.

I try to follow it all with my eyes but it's impossible.

"Is... is your brother home?"

"Oh he exploded. Jk. Lol. He's in the back," replies a vortex of emojis.

"I'm... going to check on your brother," I blurt out as I feel a madness overtaking me.

"Understandable! Have a nice day!" says the floating emojis and emerging cat pictures. He resumes "typing" on his iPhone, without using or having thumbs. I flee into the next room.

And that's where I found you, son; all swirling pages and story-data. I doubt you remember me as other than just another story you're reading, with all those stories you've read cycling within you. Your true memories are jumbled up with characters and backgrounds and plots, and you've forgotten your own real name. You want to scroll back the pages and look for it, but does it matter? You matter. Whoever those stories make you believe you are now...

Because I'm your cardboard father, and I'm home to play a board game with you. Maybe you'll remember me. Maybe you'll remember yourself. Or maybe you just think I'm another story you're reading now. That's okay. These rules are short, concise, and well written. Board games like me are good excuses to spend time together. Read my rules, if it makes you feel better. If it helps you remember who you really are.

―――――

Anthony Snider is a graphic designer in Saint Louis. 'You are What You Do' is his first published story.

We hope you have enjoyed this collection of stories. If you would like to have one of your own stories considered for the next volume of *Tabletop Tales*, please contact the editor at skdinning.co.uk or the website/blog *Ticket to Carcassonne*.

Printed in Great Britain
by Amazon